BRISCOE'S THE NAME
MURDER'S THE GAME

Introducing Sam Briscoe, a reporter who loves good booze, fast cars and beautiful women. Sam's women are as beautiful and sleek as Red Emma, the Jaguar XJ-S with V-12 engine he sprung for after a big score at the black jack tables of Vegas. Sam can down the John Jameson with anyone in the house. And he can survive a belt on the head that would retire a light heavyweight contender. You'll love Sam. His style. His savvy. His tough humor. And his street-smart skill at breaking the biggest stories around.

Golden Apple Books by Pete Hamill

THE GUNS OF HEAVEN
THE DEADLY PIECE

Dirty
Laundry

Pete Hamill

GOLDEN APPLE PUBLISHERS

DIRTY LAUNDRY
A Golden Apple Publication / June 1985

Golden Apple is a trademark of Golden Apple Publishers

ISBN 0-553-19832-7

PRINTED IN THE UNITED STATES OF AMERICA

H   0 9 8 7 6 5 4 3 2 1

This book is for my Daughter
DEIDRE

Do I sound dramatic? Off the beam?

—JACK RUBY,
June 7, 1964

Dirty
Laundry

1

I was lying on the couch in the loft, watching the fresh snow gather on the panes of the skylight and listening to Charlie Parker play "Ornithology," when the phone rang.

The button was blinking on the second line so I didn't answer it. That's the number I give to magazine editors and politicians and for them I am never home. At least not the first time they call. Besides, Bird was riding into the old sad geometries, pulling me back to a New York that wasn't there anymore. I waited for the service to pick up. They were supposed to pick up after three rings. They picked up on the ninth. By then, I was back in the Cedar Bar in some lost year in the Fifties, when everybody talked about Pollock and bop, and the painters stood beside the poets at the bar, and the girls came out of the cold of University Place with snow melting on the shoulders of their camel's hair coats and everybody I knew was young, including me.

The phone rang again. This time it was the main line and I picked it up.

"Yeah?"

"Mr. Briscoe, it's the service. Sorry to bother you, you know, but a Miss Fletcher called on the second line and she, uh, sounded like it was urgent. She was, uh, *upset.*"

"Anne Fletcher?"

"Uh, that's right. She said you knew her. She said you were old friends."

"She leave a number?"

"She did. She said she'd be there another half hour."

1

I wrote the number on a pad beside the phone, thanked the operator, and hung up.

Anne Fletcher.

Jesus Christ.

I flipped the pencil into the fireplace and went to the kitchen and dropped some ice into a frosted glass. I poured some John Jameson over the ice and splashed it with some water and took a pretty good belt, listened to the music, drained the glass, and then did it again.

Six years was a long time. If you were fighting a war. Or building a house. Or painting a picture. It wasn't very long at all if it involved kicking the memory of a woman. But after a long time I had finally kicked Anne Fletcher, the way some people kick cigarettes, and others kick smack. Cold turkey is never pleasant, not if you've come to love the habit. But I had done it. Of course there were times, off in some strange place, when her face would come to me at an odd hour of the night. Or I would pass a store window and see a book we'd read together and argued about, and I would remember fragments of sentences, verbal parries, ferocious thrusts, vicious one-liners, and the laughter later. Or I would see a woman strolling Fifth Avenue on a day crisp with spring, shiny brown hair bouncing as she walked, and I would move more quickly, rehearsing the words of greeting in my head, writing the dialogue, rewriting it, trying out the lines; until I passed the woman and it wasn't Anne Fletcher. It wasn't ever Anne Fletcher. Anne Fletcher was in Europe. Or Acapulco. Or out on the Coast. Anne Fletcher was gone off. Anne Fletcher was just another girl I used to know.

Goddamn her.

I went back to the living room. The record had finished playing, so I turned on WRVR and listened to Clark Terry play "Air Mail Special" for a while, and had some more of the Jameson, and walked to the front of the loft, and looked out at the snow as it fell steadily through the grimy alleys of SoHo. Then I went back to the phone, looked at the pad and dialed the number. After two rings, someone picked it up, but didn't say hello.

"Annie?" A pause. Nothing. "Annie, it's Sam Briscoe."

"Oh, Sam. Thank God you called. I've been trying to find you for two days."

It was her voice all right, and she wasn't in good shape.

"Two days, huh?" I didn't mention the six years, but I thought about them. "Well, what's up?"

"I've got to see you, Sam."

"I don't think that's such a good idea, Annie. What's done is done."

"It's got nothing to do with that, or with us, Sam," she said. Her voice still sounded the way it always did, as if she were trying to disrobe you, purring and sibilant, an instrument of seduction fashioned in the Iowa School of Proper Young Ladies. "I'm in trouble."

"Look in the classified section of *The Voice*, Annie. They have clinics for everything these days."

"I'm not in that kind of trouble."

"Then try a shrink."

I could sense her swallowing hard on the other end of the line. Then softly: "Wow, Sam. You really are bitter."

"Nah, I'm not bitter. I'm thirty-eight."

I was trying to tell her to hang up and get out of my life, but she wouldn't listen.

"Sam, I'm scared to death."

There was a thin wire of panic in her voice, and I said, more softly now: "Tell me what it's about."

"I can't talk on the phone."

"So. It's about money."

"Money. Banks. A killing." She paused. "But I can't explain over the phone. I've got the proof. I've got the papers. I just can't talk." Another pause.

"They're everywhere, you know. If they haven't bugged my phone, then they've bugged yours for sure. They can do anything. They can get anyone . . ."

She sounded as if she'd contracted a good dose of second-grade old-fashioned galloping paranoia.

"Who are *they?*"

"Can I meet you somewhere and tell you?"

"It's snowing out, love."

"Do you still go to that place on First Avenue?"

She meant Billy's, near 52nd Street. We'd had dinner there the first night we'd slept together.

"I go there once in a while, Annie."

"Meet me there."

"Jesus, Annie, it's already ten o'clock."

"Please, Sam. I can be there in half an hour."

I tried to sound weary and busy, but I didn't really mean it.

"Okay. Billy's, on First Avenue and 52nd Street. At eleven."

"See you," she said.

And hung up.

2

I decided to leave Red Emma home and make my way uptown by cab. Red Emma is a car. A beautiful, sleek Jaguar XJ-5, with V-12 engine, eye-level warning light array, precision cast aluminum inlet manifolds, and the temperament of a chorus girl. She and the loft were the products of The Week of the Big Score. One week I was in Saigon, with $6,500 in expense money from a certain magazine, waiting for the North Vietnamese tanks to smash down the gates of the Presidential Palace. The following week I was in Vegas. The war was finally over and I wasn't going to see any dead people in that part of the world for a long long time and I was alone and happy and started shooting craps. When I left Vegas three days later I had $108,000 in my pocket and had permanently retired from gambling. My first day home I bought Red Emma in a place on 57th Street and then realized there were very few places in the city where I could park her without kids carving their names into her shoulder blades. So I found The Loft, down on Spring Street in the neighborhood called SoHo. It's a good neighborhood, a run-down grimy place where all the bankrupt 19th-century factory buildings have started to fill up with painters and sculptors and a few writers. The restaurants are good, the saloons are peaceful, and you can walk to the Village or to the Bowery depending upon how you feel that day about the nature of the human race. I picked my building because it has a freight elevator, run by a guy named Chamaco, that takes all of Red Emma. At night I park her in my living room.

The trouble with Red Emma is that she's a thor-

oughbred. She doesn't run well on a lousy track. Rain
slows her, and snow stops her completely. So with the
snow falling heavily I walked over to West Broadway
and caught a cab.

"It's a bitch out there," the cab driver said.

"Yeah."

"It's a real son of a bitch."

"It is."

"If I didn't own this rig I'd pull it in."

"Shitty weather for driving, all right."

"I been in Brooklyn. I don't get that Brooklyn.
Twenty years I been driving and I don't get that
Brooklyn. I don't get where anything is. I don't get
the people."

"I'm from Brooklyn."

"Sorry. But you know what I mean. Even in
Brooklyn they don't get Brooklyn."

"You're not gonna tell me that only the dead
know Brooklyn, are you?"

"What?"

"Nothing. A dumb thing some writer said once."

Billy's hadn't changed. It was one of those small
excellent New York restaurants that had never been
taken up by a clique, and so had never had the bad
fortune of being ruined. People ate there who had
eaten there thirty years ago, and nothing could happen to wreck it except its sale to some corporate
gang of restaurant managers. The windows were
steamy, the tables crowded, and the decor was still
all chased mirrors, mahogany paneling, red and white
checkered tablecloths, sawdust on the floor and Yugo-
slav waiters. The steaks were good and the cole slaw
was the best on earth. I don't know why, but I hadn't
been there for a long time. The bar was jammed with
people waiting for tables.

"Mister Briscoe!"

Yuri came at me from the kitchen, his hand out
in greeting, his hair thinner, looking heavier in one of
the small golden jackets the waiters all wear there.
He acted as if the crowd at the bar didn't exist.

"Hello, Yuri."

"It's been a long time," he said, smiling a broad Slavic smile.

"Too long. Do you have a table?"

"You alone?"

"I'm expecting someone."

He looked pleased. "Two, then."

His eyes darted around the crowded restaurant. An elderly couple was getting up from a table against the back wall. The man held the woman's chair, and helped her on with her coat. They seemed to like each other. It was that kind of place.

"It'll be just a minute," Yuri said.

"Fine."

"Where you been?"

"Oh, around," I said. "Mostly out of town."

"You don't write for the paper anymore?"

"Nah, Yuri."

"How come?"

"Too old. I retired."

"Too old? I'm too old. You're not too old."

"Reporters are people who get sent places to be pushed around by the cops, Yuri. I'm too old for that."

He laughed and led me to the table.

"John Jameson with a splash, right?"

"You do have a memory, Yuri."

He went to the bar and I sat with my back against the wall, staring at the Fresh Bay Scallops sign, and wondering why I was there.

An hour later I was on my fourth Jameson and Anne Fletcher still hadn't shown up. I had left the number on the pad beside the phone and no Anne Fletcher was listed in the Manhattan, Brooklyn or Queens telephone books. I didn't try the Bronx; nobody lives in the Bronx anymore. And if she had been in Staten Island she would have said so; to Anne Fletcher living in Staten Island would have been like settling in Kenya. She could not have kept it a secret.

Ten minutes before the kitchen closed, I ordered a medium sirloin and some extra cole slaw and an-

other Irish and tried to fight down my anger. She
was late. But then she had always been late, and
there was no reason to think she'd changed. She was
even late for breakfast when she served it in bed and
she was always late for parties and she had never
seen the first ten minutes of any Broadway show.
The first couple of months we were together I thought
the lateness was part of her act. She wanted to be
an actress then; all the young women wanted to be
actresses then, to become someone else at least once a
day, in her case someone who hadn't grown up in
Iowa with a pain in the ass mother and a drunken
insurance man father. I first thought that she had
read in some fan magazine that Marilyn Monroe was
always late, so if she was going to be a big famous
actress then she would have to start being late too.
But it was more than that. Anne Fletcher was one of
those girls out of the great Midwest who were
knocked permanently off-center the day they arrived
in New York and never fully recovered. She was so
goddamned beautiful that I learned to relax and forget the lateness, and so did everyone else who knew
her. She was so goddamned beautiful I should have
known the day I met her that she would end up
breaking my goddamned heart.

I ate the steak in silence, watching the snow fall
on First Avenue. There is no jukebox in Billy's and
no strolling musicians and no television set, so the
sounds are always human: people murmuring, com-
plaining, lying, seducing, consoling. But it was late
now and the place was starting to empty. The parked
cars in the street were crowned by two inches of
snow. I finished the steak and ordered an Irish coffee.

Then I remembered the answering service. I don't
know why I hadn't thought of it earlier; the Irish part
of me is slow. They had taken her number. They
might still have a record of it. I went to the bar,
broke a dollar for change, went to the wall phone and
dialed the service. There were six fresh calls for me,
but none from Anne Fletcher. I asked them to look

around for the number she had left earlier. They found it. This time I looked at it more carefully. It was a Brooklyn exchange.

I dialed. The line was busy.

I went back to the table and sipped the Irish coffee. It had cooled off and tasted too sweet now and very thick. I'd have to do a hundred pushups to work off half the meal.

I dialed again. Still busy.

I asked Yuri to bring me a brandy, with some soda and ice on the side. He looked at me with something like pity, but he didn't say anything. Maybe something really had happened to her. Money. Banks. A killing. And, of course, the ever-present "they." Every nut who ever called a city desk after midnight said "they" were after him. But Annie had papers. Sweet Annie had proof. It sounded like one of those lousy Fifties movies she wanted so desperately to be part of, years ago, when we were young.

I dialed again and this time it rang through.

"Hello? Who is speaking?"

A husky female voice with a faint Latin accent.

"Who's this?" I said.

"Who is this?" she said.

"I want to talk to Anne Fletcher."

"Who *are* you?"

"Hey, what the hell is this? An interrogation?"

She hung up.

I stared at the receiver and then looked around. Yuri and another waiter were watching me sadly.

I dialed again.

"Hello? Who is speaking?"

"Listen, I'm sorry," I said. "You have nothing to do with this. But I've been waiting for Anne Fletcher for more than two hours. It's snowing out and I'm half-drunk and pissed-off and didn't really want to see her in the first place, and I just want to find out what the hell is going on."

"Oh, my God. You must be the reporter."

"Briscoe's the name."

"Oh, my God. *Ay Dios mio.*"

Her voice drifted away.

"Hey, what is going *on?* Where's Anne?"

"It's too late," she said. "It's all too late."

"Too late for what?"

"For Anna. She's dead."

3

All the way to Brooklyn in the cab, I thought about what I had been told. A couple of hours ago Anne Fletcher was alive, panicky and scared on a telephone, calling for help. And now she was dead. A crash on the Brooklyn Bridge, said the oddly disembodied Latin voice on the phone. And here I was on the same bridge and there were no police cars, no ambulances, no signs saying Here Died Anne Fletcher. Just an empty bridge on a snowy night in New York.

The voice on the phone belonged to one Moya Vargas and she said she shared an apartment with Anne Fletcher on Columbia Heights, a fine block overlooking the harbor. I paid the driver and overtipped him because of the weather and the empty hack he would pull back to Manhattan. Then I went up the stoop of 141 and rang the bell that said Vargas. I held the handle of the inside door waiting for a buzzer to let me in. I waited a while and then rang the bell again. The door was one of those rich jobs that click instead of buzzing. I went inside and the hall was very quiet. The stairs were carpeted. I started up.

On the top floor, there were three doors. One of them opened a crack and I could see a liquid eye staring out.

"Briscoe?"

"Yeah."

She took a chain off the door and let me in.

"Please come in."

She had a long oval face, with taut skin pulled over high cheekbones. Her eyes were very black

11

and widely spaced. Her hair was parted in the middle, worn so severely that a white line of scrubbed scalp sliced down the middle. The hair was glossy and fresh. She was wearing a crisp white blouse and black slacks and a pair of red Oriental slippers. Her breasts moved when she did. She wore a small gold cross at her neck. She was beautiful.

"Can I get you a drink?" she said in the husky accented voice.

"I've had enough for one night. A glass of water, maybe, or . . ."

"Coffee?"

"Beautiful."

She went into the tiny kitchenette. The apartment was one of those standard two-bedroom things, with fairly standard girls-living-together furniture. Only the prints on the walls were special. They were by Cuevas and Rafael Coronel and there were several beautiful drawings by Zuñiga. I drifted over to the open kitchen door.

"Are you Mexican?" I asked her.

"Why do you ask?" she said from the kitchen. The dry coffee smelled strong as she spooned it into a paper filter wedged into a Chemex.

"The drawings and the prints. They're all from Mexico."

"Have you been to Mexico?"

"*Cuando fue un niño,*" I said, trying to smile. Her face brightened.

"*Habla español?*" she said, in a surprised voice.

"A little. I went to school in Mexico on the GI Bill, a hundred years ago." She let that register and turned back to the stove. She did not look comfortable at a stove.

The water boiled and she poured it through the filter. While it dripped through, she opened a closet door and took out two cups. I walked away from the kitchen and stood at the picture window and looked out at the harbor. The lights of the skyline were dimmed by the falling snow. Over to the left, the Statue of Liberty looked like a small green toy, lost in a distant fog.

"Cream and sugar?" she said. There was less accent in her voice now. The phone always amplifies it. She poured the coffee out of the Chemex into a silver pot and put the pot, the cups, sugar and cream on a silver tray.

"Black," I said. "No sugar."

She put the tray down on a cocktail table and sat in a large winged chair. I sat on the couch.

"Okay," I said. "What happened?"

She stared at the cup. "I only know what the police told me," she said slowly. "There was an accident on the Brooklyn Bridge. The car . . . it hit the guard rail on the inside lane. Then it got turned around and went across to the other side before stopping. When they got there she was dead. They think her neck was broken."

"Any witnesses?"

"Nobody was crazy enough to be on that bridge in the snow except Annie."

"You think she was crazy?"

"She was . . . upset."

"But what about crazy?"

"She was afraid. She was very . . . afraid. Of something . . . someone. Maybe she was a little crazy. . . . She spent two days trying to find you."

She said the last sentence sharply, as if what had happened was somehow my fault.

"I didn't know that, Miss Vargas."

"Of course. How could you?"

"Two days . . ." I said. "Why?"

"Why what?"

"Why did she want to see me?"

"I don't know. Something to do with the bank."

"What bank?"

"The New York Bank and Trust Company. She worked there."

"Anne Fletcher worked in a *bank?*"

She smiled thinly. "I suppose it seems . . . strange —for Anne. She had only worked there six or seven months. Because of her boyfriend."

"Which one?"

"The young one. The son."

"The son of who?"

"The young one's name was Pepe. He wasn't so young, I guess. Pepe was young only compared to his father. They owned the bank."

I laughed. "A guy named *Pepe* owns a bank in New York? What was it? A numbers bank?"

She didn't smile. "They are very rich. Pepe was going to get everything. Until the accident."

"You've lost me. Anne's accident? Or was Pepe in an accident too?"

"Pepe was killed in a plane crash last week. In the mountains outside Acapulco."

I took another sip of the coffee.

"I didn't see anything in the papers about the owner of a New York bank dying in a crash in Mexico."

"Nobody knew he owned the bank. That's one of the things Anne had just learned. That's one reason why she was so scared."

I finished the coffee and stood up. She sat as if clenched by the chair, holding the coffee cup and the saucer very tightly, while rivers of tension ran under the taut skin.

"Listen," I said, "there's something wrong about all of this." I stared at her a long moment. "Why don't you tell me the whole story from the beginning?"

"The beginning? Where do I start? I told the police everything I know."

"The police were here?"

"Two detectives. A man named Kelly."

"Charlie Kelly?"

She shrugged in a stiff way. "Maybe. I only remember Kelly."

"Why don't you tell me what you told them? Starting with when you met Annie."

She poured herself another cup of coffee from the silver pot, and dropped in three fat cubes of sugar.

"I met her seven or eight months ago. In that place on First Avenue. Maxwell's Plum? She came in alone. She was very tanned. She stood next to me at the bar and I asked her where she got the tan and she told me Acapulco and one thing led to another, talking about Mexico, and we stayed together at the bar, fighting off the animals."

"The bar at Maxwell's Plum isn't exactly a place for peace and quiet."

"I know. But that night I wanted to see faces, to see people, even to see animals, as long as they didn't drag me off with them. She was nervous that night too, looking around every time the door opened, as if she were afraid of being caught, I don't know by whom. And she started to tell me about Pepe, and how she had met him a year before in Acapulco, and how she had been having an affair with him, off and on, and how jealous he was, and how violent. And she was asking me what she should do about it, because she thought a Latin woman would know how to handle him."

She was talking easily and quickly now, and the tension had drained out of her.

"What did you tell her?"

"I told her to get rid of him."

"That was sensible. Too sensible for our Annie."

"She said that Pepe was paying for her apartment, somewhere in the seventies, the lease was in his name, and she didn't have a job, and didn't know how she could get rid of him. She said Pepe would kill her if she left him. I understood. I knew the type. And she was right. They are pussycats with their mothers and take it out on their girl friends."

"*Los supermachos.*"

"*Exactamente.* Do you want a brandy?"

I looked at my watch. It was 2:15.

"What the hell."

"I've got some Carlos Primero here somewhere."

She went to the bar against the wall. I watched her long strong legs move tautly under the black slacks.

"I met her the next day for lunch. She wasn't working and I was working for a lawyer who was in the import-export business and was never in the office. That was why I went a little crazy every once in a while. Being in that office alone." She opened the brandy bottle and produced two fresh glasses.

"How come you're not married?" I said.

"I was. A long time ago. How about you?"

"The same."

"Before your affair with Anne?"

"Practically before puberty."

"Children?"

"A daughter. She's in boarding school in Switzerland."

"Really? Where?"

"A place called Beau Soleil. The far end of the lake, in a town called Villars."

Her face brightened. "I know Villars. The skiing is marvelous, up above Vevey. Do you ski?"

"I barely walk, Miss Vargas. Finish the story."

She handed me the brandy. It was her turn to look out at the snow.

"We met at lunch and became friends. She had a hard life. A few too many men. A few too many abortions. She wanted to be an actress."

"I know."

"But she never really worked at it. I told her she should get a job, for a salary. I told her she had to become independent, that she couldn't live off men, and if she broke the habit of living off men then maybe she could find a man she could really live *with*. I guess nobody ever told her that before."

"I did. Once. She didn't want to hear it."

The brandy was very warm as it moved through me.

"Well, maybe she wasn't ready then. You loved her, didn't you?"

"I guess."

"She didn't know what to do about love. She told me once that when her parents died she didn't know what to do. There was nobody left who really loved her for herself."

"That sounds like bad *Photoplay*."

"You heard it before?"

"Some of it. I heard about how the parents died. Not from her. From a newspaper. It came over the wires one night while I was writing a column in the city room and somebody remembered that I used to go out with a girl named Fletcher and came over and showed me the piece about the car going off a bridge in a flood in Iowa or someplace. I guess that family had bad luck with bridges. Anyway, I knew she didn't really like either the mother or the father, and she'd be feeling guilty as hell. I wanted to call her up and talk to her but I didn't know where she was."

"She was in Spain. With a man. She didn't hear about it until a month later, and they were already buried and forgotten."

"Shit."

I went over to the bar and poured myself another brandy. I gave her a look that said, "What happened?"

"Well, she must have been ready, because one night she showed up downstairs with a U-Haul-It. Is that how you say it? U-Haul-It?"

"Yes."

"She had moved all of her things out of his apartment. She didn't have much. Clothes and a few books. Well, I had the extra room and she moved in with me. She went to work at the bank the next week."

"What did she do there?" I said.

"She was in the bookkeeping department. It turned out that she had a talent for numbers."

"Anne Fletcher had a talent for numbers? You're kidding."

"Well, she did. She just had never used this talent before, I suppose."

"And Pepe owned the bank?"

Her face was cautious. "Not then."

"You mean he tracked her down and bought the whole goddamned bank, just to get his hands on her again?"

"I don't know. All I know is that she was happy for a while. She was reading books and watching television a lot and started going to Broadway shows and liked the job. She liked that it was regular, you know? Nine to five. And she liked that she was getting paid for her work. She had three raises in six months and was . . . moving up the ladder? She stayed out of the East Side, out of the places where she might meet Pepe, and she didn't see very many other men."

"What does that mean?"

"A few people from work. Young men. Her age."

"That wasn't so young any more, was it?"

"She was young, if you're forty."

"Are you forty?"

"I wouldn't tell you if I was." She smiled a coy, actress-like smile.

"When did Pepe show up again?"

"A month ago. Anne told me he just walked into the bank one day, followed by a lot of accountants and other businessmen. The head of the bank came out to greet him and they all went to the offices upstairs. And he saw her. Pepe saw her sitting at a desk, and he nodded very formally, she told me, and kept going. That night, when she left work there was a limousine waiting for her and it started all over again. She began to stay out all night. And when she was here she seemed jumpy and afraid. The phone would ring and she would jump. She lost weight."

"It's what the more simple-minded shrinks call a regression."

"*Claro*. Then last week she came home and there were bruises on her body."

"Goddamnit."

"But still she went to the bank. And this time it was different. She was angry, but she was . . . how you say? Cool?"

"*Sí*, cool."

"She started bringing home papers from the bank. She said this time she would do the hurting."

"What kind of papers?"

"Numbers. Figures. Letters. All Xerox copies."

"Where are they now?"

"She took them with her tonight. To give to you. A lot of papers."

I walked over to one of the bedroom doors.

"Is this hers?"

"The other one. The police already looked through it."

"Did you tell them what you told me?"

"Not all of it."

"Why not?"

"They didn't ask."

"They never do."

Anne's room was small, with satin sheets, and a thick Mexican-style blanket folded neatly at the foot of the bed. The drapes were closed. It was very warm. On one wall, there was a handsomely mounted reproduction of the Paul Davis poster of Che Guevara. Below Che-as-Christ there was a small bookcase. Most of it was standard fare: a Rona Jaffe novel, *The Other Side of Midnight*, a few books on yoga and physical fitness, *The Godfather*, the Manchester book on Jack Kennedy. There were two books on Fidel Castro, and I remembered how she never had given up her romantic vision of Fidel and the revolution. She was a

17-year-old college freshman that New Year's Day when Batista packed the gold into the C-47, and Fidel and Che and the others came down from the mountains. She and a girl friend had pooled their money and bought tickets for Havana, and roamed the streets with the bearded ones for weeks, laughing at the Castro Convertibles who were burning Batista's picture in the stove and cheering sheepishly for Fidel. It must have been a hell of a party. She used to have a picture from that time, taken at some great rally showing her with Che and Raul Castro and the one called Camilio Cienfuegos, who later was killed in a plane crash. She was young and bouncy and unbelievably beautiful, and if she was seventeen that year, then she was no longer young when she died. Later, the revolution started to really happen, and this time it was not a simple matter of some fat slug replacing another fat slug in the customs job; this was a revolution, and it was to be made by Cubans, and there was no place in it for daughters of the American middle class like Anne Fletcher. So she had come home and all she had to show for that giddy time was that photograph. But the picture wasn't there in the apartment in Brooklyn. Two others stood in frames on top of the bureau. One was of her parents, standing outside a white frame house in some forgotten town; I had seen the picture before, on top of a bureau on 30th Street. The other showed her sitting with a group at a table in the sunshine. Beside her was a heavy-set moustached man, with powerful arms rippling under a sport shirt. He was wearing sunglasses. The place looked like a terrace bar in Acapulco.

"Is this Pepe?" I said, pointing to the moustached man.

"*Eso es.*"

"He doesn't look like her type."

"Maybe not," Moya said. "But we'll never know, will we?"

"He crashed into a *mountain?*"

"In a private plane. Pepe, a pilot, and that's all."

I looked through the bureau drawers. Underwear and blouses and sweaters were stacked in neat piles but there were no papers, no letters, not a trace of anything in her life. Except for the picture with Pepe, she had left absolutely nothing behind her that could have proved her existence.

"How did you hear that Pepe had crashed?"

"She told me. She was very upset."

"How did she find out?"

"I . . . I don't know."

I picked up the photograph and looked at it again. Most of the people were Mexicans, and Annie looked like the classic vacationing *gringita:* the big white smile, the hair lighter from the sun, her skin dark against a coarse white Mexican peasant blouse. She was not wearing a bra; she never did, even before it was fashionable.

"Can I take this?"

"Porqué no?"

"And I need the phone for a little while."

"Of course."

She went back to the kitchen while I used the phone to find Kelly of the Homicide Squad. I didn't try Homicide. I tried P. J. Clarke's and he was there.

"Charlie, it's Briscoe."

"Well, I'll be damned, the Irish Hebe. What the hell do you want?"

"Some information."

"I thought you quit the paper. At least I was hoping you'd quit the paper." His voice was a little burry with whiskey.

"It's about a friend. Her name was Anne Fletcher. She was killed on the Brooklyn Bridge tonight. I heard you had the squeal."

Now his voice was cautious. "What about it?"

"I want to know if it could have been murder."

"Strictly an accident, Briscoe. You know how that goddamn bridge gets when it's wet. It's those ridiculous metal grids. You couldn't cross that goddamn thing safely on skis."

"Where on the bridge did it happen, Charlie?"

"The Manhattan side about a hundred yards before you reach the end and get the ramp to the East River Drive."

"You're sure it's an accident?"

"Yeah."

There was a lot of noise in the background.

"Where's the car?"

"Down at the Elizabeth Street station. Why?"

"I just want to look at it."

"Don't play sleuth, Briscoe. I'm the sleuth. You're the reporter."

"Tell me, sleuth, were there any papers in the car?"

"There was nothing in the car but her."

"What about a handbag?"

"Not even that. Just her. We found a wallet with credit cards and a driver's license in the glove compartment. But we didn't get there right away. We don't have too many guys loose since the budget cuts, Briscoe. Especially for traffic accidents."

"In other words, somebody could have copped the handbag?"

"In this town, any goddamn thing is possible. What else?"

"You could call Elizabeth Street for me, Charlie. Tell them I want to look at the car."

"You're interrupting my social life."

"You know us Hebes, Charlie. Always pushing."

He grunted and hung up. Then I called Pete Jacobs at St. Rocco's in the Village. He is one of the last priests in New York who make house calls. I gave him the details and asked him to arrange a funeral.

When I was finished, Moya Vargas was coming across the living room from the kitchen carrying a platter of scrambled eggs and English muffins.

"Well, I'll be damned."

"It's cold outside," she said.

"I used to know a song like that."

"So did I. We used to sing it in boarding school."

4

The car was a 1975 Chevrolet and the snow was beginning to cover it in the parking lot of the Elizabeth Street station. A moustached young cop stood beside me in the lot, his raincoat slick with melted snow.

"You a cop, or what?" he said.

"Reporter."

"Oh, yeah? What paper?"

"Freelance."

"You mean for magazines and stuff?"

"Yeah. Were you on when this thing came in?"

I was brushing snow off the car. The side door was smashed in, the front windshield was shattered, there was broken glass and blood on the seat covers. She must have been a mess.

"Nah. That was the four to twelve. Hey, I write a little myself."

"That's good. What do you write?"

"Ah, different things." He seemed embarrassed. "You know . . ."

"Poetry, right?"

"How did you know?"

The gas cap was missing, probably dislodged in the crash.

"You seemed ashamed of it."

"Ah, you know what it's like. You write poems, they think you're a fag. But I like it. You ever hear of this guy Andrew Marvell?"

"Yeah. He's good."

He started to recite: " 'Had we but world enough, and time . . .' "

One of the tires was flattened, the rubber rudely torn, obviously not sliced.

25

"You ever write any poetry?" the cop said.

"I committed a few poems in my golden youth."

"Who did you like?"

"Marvell was pretty good. I liked John Donne too. And Shakespeare sure knew what the hell he was doing."

"The sonnets. Yeah, he was beautiful."

Then I saw what I was looking for. The left rear fender had a dent in it. The polished surface of the paint was broken, but not rusted. Something had recently banged it from behind.

"Well thanks, pal," I said.

"You're finished?"

"For tonight."

"Hey, it was nice talking to you," the poet said.

"Keep writing," I said, and went out of the lot to find a cab.

There were three rewrite men in the city room of the *Post* when I walked in a half-hour later. Harvey Matofsky was on the desk. The wet snow had pasted my hair to my skull, and I was starting to need a shave. Harvey looked up and blinked, as if he'd just seen a trunk murderer make an entrance.

"What the hell happened to you?" he said.

"I went out for a walk."

"From where? Buffalo?"

"Elizabeth Street. You can't get a cab anywhere tonight, even if you're white."

Harvey's face twitched; it's what he uses for a smile.

"What's up, Sam?"

"I need to look at some clips, Harve."

He reached into his desk, poked around, and found the key to the library. They didn't staff the place at night and even the reporters had to help themselves to the clips.

Harvey said: "You know how it works? B follows A, C follows B. This is called alphabetical order."

"Left to right or up and down?"

"In that place, you never can tell."

I thanked him and walked down the hall toward the library. The three rewrite men never moved. I stopped in the men's room and washed my face. Fatigue was seeping through me like a bad gas. I never had a lot of hair, but looking at myself in the men's room mirror I was sure that I'd lost more of it in the last eight hours.

There were no clips on Moya Vargas. I wasn't even sure that was her name. I wasn't very sure that the story she had told me was true, and I didn't like the way she shifted from grief to scrambled eggs without many stops in between. But some of her story began to seem plausible. Pepe's full name was Jose Luis Fuentes. There were a lot of envelopes of clips under that name. Maybe forty of them. Most of them were about guys from East Harlem who had split their wives open with axes, in arguments over Francisco Someone.

But in the last envelope there was something about a Jose Luis Fuentes who had been killed in a plane crash.

The clip was eleven days old.

It was from the *Wall Street Journal*.

Acapulco, Dec. 12 (AP)—The son of a prominent Mexican banker was killed today when his private jet crashed into a mountain 35 miles from this resort city.

Jose Luis Fuentes, 37, was traveling to Acapulco from Houston when the plane lost contact with the airport here.

Fuentes was the son of Luis Fuentes y Aragon, owner of the Banco de Maya, headquartered in Mexico City. He is survived by a wife and three children.

The pilot of the Lear jet also perished in the crash.

That was all. It wasn't much but at least it convinced me that Pepe Fuentes actually had existed. The clip did not mention Anne Fletcher, or a guy who beat up women, or long sultry weekends in Aca-

pulco. It also did not mention the New York Bank
and Trust Company. But there had been a Pepe
Fuentes.

I slipped the clip into my wallet, replaced all
the Fuentes envelopes in their file drawer and then
went to the next aisle and took down the envelopes
on the New York Bank and Trust. A lot of these clips
were those rehashed press releases that pass for news
on the business page of the *New York Times*. But
I began to pick up a pattern.

The New York Bank and Trust was clearly a political bank. That is to say, at least three Democratic
county leaders were on the board, along with the Republican leader of a suburban county. The rest of
the board was made up of the names that always
appear in agate type as campaign contributors after
an election is over. These are real estate operators,
stock market wiseguys, and various businessmen who
find it profitable to invest in a mayor. An article from
Barron's said that 78 percent of the company's stock
was owned by a holding company in Geneva called
the Intercontinental Trade Company, but clearly the
bank was a resting place for political power brokers.
There were obvious advantages to being a political
bank, although none of that information was in the
clips. A political bank usually had more deposits from
state and city agencies than other banks did. A well-
connected political bank set up mortgages and loans
for the big builders and real estate people, and was
rewarded with political business. For example, the
millions that are paid out in welfare can be kept in a
political bank, to be used as a revolving fund for
the people who own the bank, with the bank profit-
ing from the steady turnover of deposits and pay-
outs. The bankers also have friends in the stock market and the insurance business who usually give their
stock and insurance business to their friends. It works
the same way with politicians. This is called the
free enterprise system.

I made a lot of notes from the clips, and then

went over to the picture file. I found photographs of
the bank's principal officers—two strapping Protestants named Martin Caldwell and Dennis Sherman
—flanking Nelson Rockefeller at some Republican
dinner. There were formal, lifeless Bachrach portraits
of the same principals. That was all. Then I checked
Standard and Poor's. The New York Bank and Trust
was the twenty-fourth largest bank in the United
States, with a capitalization of $80,000,000. On paper
it was a legitimate outfit. Nowhere in the clips, in
the photo file or in the reference books was there any
mention of Jose Luis Fuentes except for the notice of
his death.

I heard the door open and looked around. Harvey
was standing there with a piece of wire copy in his
hand. His face was even more ashen than usual. I
knew what the wire copy must be about. He walked
over, without looking at what I was doing, and
handed me the copy. All about an accident in the
snow on the Brooklyn Bridge. I took it, folded it, and
slipped it into my jacket pocket.

"It's a great thing, this life business," he said.

"It certainly is."

5

I waited outside 63 Wall Street for more than half
an hour while most of the city of New York went to
work. Cars were mashing the fallen snow into slush
in the streets. The chestnut vendors were already set
up, and one lone hotdog guy pushed his cart and
umbrella around the corner of Broad Street. I read
the *News*, which had run nothing about the accident,
and watched the young girls come up from the sub-
way, their hair in curlers, while little puffs of steam
drifted from their mouths as they talked to their young
men. At a little after nine, a cab pulled up and Al
Quinn got out. He looked at me and his face fell.

"Ah, shit, Briscoe," he said. "What the hell do
you want?"

"Information."

"I thought it was gonna be a nice day. I thought
I could sit in my office with the door open and
watch my secretary's ass and have a nice rich lunch
and read the papers and make a few bucks. I didn't
have you on the schedule."

"It's important, Al."

He looked at my clothes, and I followed him
through the revolving door.

"You smell like a bastard," he said.

"Stay upwind."

"Can we talk on the roof?"

"There's an ape up there with a girl in his hand."

"Not this building. That's crosstown."

I smiled. "You look rich, Al."

"I *am* rich, fuckhead. I am richer than you. I am
richer than any former U. S. Attorney in the United
States."

"Things are that bad, huh?"

We walked into the offices of the law firm. Everything was quiet. The downtown people liked it that way. And I suppose it makes sense. If you commit crimes with briefcases you better try to make the place look like a clergyman's parlor. He led me into a corner office. The desk was polished and clean. Liquor bottles stood discreetly in a wall cabinet. There were no photographs, only the English sporting prints they go for down there. A window opened out over the Battery, and the harbor was sparkling in the cold sun.

"Coffee?"

"Sure?"

He punched a button. "Miss Maronella, a couple of coffees."

"The Protestants keep you two Catholics together, huh?"

"It saves on Mass cards."

He looked at me and waited. I said:

"I need some help."

"It depends on what it is, Sam. Nothing illegal?"

"Perish the thought."

The secretary came in with two coffees in stoneware mugs. She was young and large-breasted, with thin legs. She looked at Quinn and something trembled in her face. She tiptoed out.

"I see, said the blind man."

"She's trying desperately to lose her virginity," Quinn said. "It's a contract I'm too old to handle, but it's nice to think about. Keeps the blood pumping."

"Yeah."

"What's the problem, Sam?"

"I want to know about a guy named Jose Luis Fuentes. Some people call him Pepe. His father owns a bank in Mexico City."

Something happened to Quinn's face. "What about him?" he said.

"Who is he? What was he doing in New York for

the last year? What is his relationship to the New York Bank and Trust Company? Things like that."

He looked at me for a long moment. Then: "I knew I should have stayed in that cab."

I stared at him. He went over and gazed at the harbor. Then he glanced wearily at his watch: "Wait outside. I've got to make a few calls."

I went out and sat on a couch in the reception room and looked at Miss Maronella's chest while thumbing through a copy of *Business Week*. Quinn was right; she kept your blood pumping. She knew I was looking at her, and alternated between blushing and stretching a little too hard to her left. The faces in *Business Week* were all the same: gray-haired, well-tanned, crinkly-eyed. The kind of people who play a lot of tennis and go straight from the nursery to the boardroom with only an occasional stop at the C.I.A. after Yale. I saw one of the lights on Miss Maronella's phone go off and on and off again and on again. Quinn was placing all the calls himself.

Then the intercom buzzed, she picked it up, and put it right down again.

"You can go in now, Mr. Briscoe."

I went in. Al was standing now, his foot on a shelf above the radiator, staring out at the harbor.

"I usually don't do this for free, Briscoe."

"You owe me a couple, Al," I said.

He sat down again behind the desk and looked at the yellow pad.

"Okay," he said. "First, you know he's dead?"

"A plane crash, right."

"Yeah, it was a private Falcon that he leased three times a month to commute to Acapulco."

"The paper said a Lear."

"As usual the paper is wrong. The plane left Houston at 12:40, and somewhere over a town called Chica Grande it exploded in a ball of flame. That was about 2:40. In the morning. The pilot's name was Arturo Hernandez. He had been flying for eleven hours. The flight started from Marine Air Terminal at LaGuardia. The Houston manifest showed that Fuentes was still on board when they left for Acapulco."

"How much does that kind of commuting cost?"

"About ten thousand dollars a trip."

"Jesus."

"The wreckage was scattered for five hundred feet, but Fuentes' body was blown clear. The family came up from Mexico City the next day and identified the remains. He was cremated the next day in Mexico City."

"Did he live in Mexico City, Acapulco, or here?"

"He had an apartment in the Olympic Towers, up on Fifth Avenue. You know, that big white elephant the Greeks built before the market collapsed. It cost him about six thousand a month. He lived there with his wife, and probably a couple of kids. My people aren't too sure about that part."

"So he was going back and forth to Acapulco to avoid taxes?"

"Probably. If he stayed out of the United States a hundred and eighty days a year, he didn't have to pay taxes here."

"What about the bank?"

"That's the funny part. Nobody really wants to talk about it." He pointed at me with a yellow pencil. "I have to keep this all off the record, Sam."

"Of course."

"Well, your man Pepe showed up in New York about a year ago. He had good credentials from Mexico, and he had letters of introduction to a lot of people. His rabbi was Frank Martin."

"Frankie the Fixer? The great Port Authority man?"

"That's him. Frank Martin introduced him around, took him to 21 and Régine's and La Cote Basque, introduced him to David Rockefeller over at Chase, found him his apartment. Pepe let it be known that he was looking to enter business in New York. Specifically the banking business. He said the Mexican economy was on its ass, the Communists were in the hills, the government was full of Lefties . . ."

"Sounds like a pretty good country."

He looked at the yellow pad. "He met a lot of the politicians through Martin, and started looking at New York Bank and Trust. He had a financial statement showing he was worth a hundred and seven million with liabilities of about five. It was, as they say, a beautiful statement. He got Struthers and Simpson to handle the deal for him."

"What deal?"

"The takeover of the bank. He was going to buy out the managing partners. So he had to get approval through the State Banking Commission. They were a little leery of it, but Struthers and Simpson was just what they wanted. A high-class outfit, with at least one former Secretary of State on the payroll. They were working very hard on the deal."

"I heard Pepe had already moved into the bank when he died."

"Right. He had an office up there. Moved in a couple of months ago when Dennis Sherman, one of the bosses, moved out and went to Florida. The deal wasn't official yet, but Fuentes was basically running the place, with another boss, a hell of a nice guy named Caldwell."

He stopped talking and put the pad down. His hands moved in and out of his pockets like a smoker's when he's mislaid his pack.

"And . . . ?"

"That's all. The sale of the bank is held up. Everything is a mess, I would imagine, since the guy crashed. That's all I could get." He sounded as if he meant what he was saying; if it wasn't the full truth, I was sure he hadn't told me any lies.

"Well," I said, "I guess I better go see this Caldwell."

He took the top sheet off the yellow pad and started tearing it into tiny pieces. "What's this about, Sam?"

"I'm not sure yet. Maybe murder."

"Yeah?"

"Forget it," I said. "You're retired. You're the richest former U. S. Attorney in the world, remember?"

"I remember."

"Well, that's a full-time job. Anyway, thanks, Al."

He came around the desk and walked me to the door.

"If you go up to see Caldwell, Sam, do yourself a favor."

"What's that?"

"Grab a bath."

"Up yours."

6

I went back to the loft and slept from 10:30 to 2. When I woke up I felt as if I'd spent a night licking pool tables. I boiled myself in the shower and then dressed. Then I went out and took a cab through the slush to the main office of the New York Bank and Trust Company on Fifth Avenue.

I walked past the long lines at the tellers' cages, and stopped at the Customer Services counter. A pale man in his late forties came over.

"I'd like to see Mr. Caldwell, please."

"Do you have an appointment, sir?"

"No, I don't."

"Well, I'm afraid . . ."

"Tell him it's Mr. Briscoe. I'm a friend of Mr. Fuentes."

His mouth said "oh" but the sound didn't come out. He went over to a phone and dialed two digits. He talked in a muffled way. Then he came back.

"Follow me, please."

He clicked open a low gate and led me to an elevator at the back of the bank. It was one of those elevators with gates that open out and room for only two people, a holdover from the old days. He closed the gates behind us and pressed three and the elevator went up.

The third floor was wood-paneled and thickly carpeted, but there were no windows, just oak doors opening off a central corridor. Each door had a secretary working at a desk outside and none of them looked up. This floor of the bank was even more muffled than the places downtown. Money seems to make all of these people want to live in cathedrals.

Caldwell was waiting for us. "Mr. Briscoe?"

"Mr. Caldwell, I presume."

"Please come in."

Caldwell opened the door to his office and the stooge from Customer Services bowed himself away. I went into another wood-paneled room; the executives of New York have laid waste entire forests to furnish their offices. Caldwell looked at me dubiously; he had blue worried eyes, thinning white hair that was red around the edges, a nose that hurt from whiskey. He was dressed in J. Press 1958 modern: narrow lapels, a vest, narrow pants, all in gray.

"You've come about Mr. Fuentes?" He made it sound as if Mr. Fuentes was a loan.

"That's right," I said brightly.

"But you're not really a friend, are you?"

"No. I never met the man."

"You're a reporter, aren't you?"

"Sort of."

"I thought I recognized the by-line. Why don't you write the column for the paper anymore?"

"It just wasn't fun reading it anymore. I decided to go home for a while."

"Are you going to write about . . . Fuentes?"

"I might."

He breathed out heavily as he sat down. His hands played with a pencil.

"Is this off the record?"

"For now," I said. "It depends what you have to tell me."

"Off the record, Fuentes was a crook," he said wearily. "We were taken. It's as simple as that. The banking commissioners were here yesterday and this morning and they'll be back tomorrow. Off the record, we've been gutted."

"How?"

"The man had impeccable credentials and we went for them," he said. His face was very sad, and his eyes were thirsty. "He was introduced to us by the best people."

"You mean Frank Martin."

He seemed surprised. "Why, yes. How did you know that?"

"I learned it. Go on."

"His financial statement was beautiful. His father's bank in Mexico is very solid. He had contacts here and in Washington. He had Struthers and Simpson to handle the sale."

"Did the sale ever go through?"

"No. It was pending."

"So how did he hit you with the sting?"

Caldwell got up and walked to a cabinet and opened a door. He found the ice bucket and dropped a single cube in a glass. Then he poured in some vodka.

"Drink?"

"Same as you. Rocks."

He poured the drinks and kept talking in his deflated, ruined way.

"One day he came in and opened eight bank accounts, in the names of eight separate companies, both here and in Mexico," he said. "They were all legitimate companies, as far as we could tell, and besides, he had that beautiful statement and those beautiful friends."

"How much did he put in the accounts?"

"Two hundred dollars each, I'm afraid."

I laughed. "Beautiful."

"I suppose, in a way, it was."

I sipped the vodka. "Let me fill in the rest," I said. "He then applied for loans against those accounts. The loans were for a lot of money, so the accounts really weren't security. But you figured, what the hell, the guy is buying the bank, and he's good for it, isn't he?"

"He had that beautiful statement," Caldwell said. The vodka was loosening his face, and he smiled.

"On top of that, you weren't sure what he would do when the sale went through. Who he would keep working here and who he would fire. So you approved the loans."

"Right. And they were absolutely unsecured."

"And now he's gone, and you're stuck for the money."

"You're clever, Mr. Briscoe."

"No. I just know a lot of thieves."

"We were taken."

"For how much?"

"A lot."

"Off the record, how much?"

He hesitated, slumped back in the leather chair. He smiled a dumb little smile.

"Forty two million dollars."

"Son of a fucking bitch."

"That's what I said," Caldwell murmured.

I got up and went to the bar and opened the vodka bottle again and filled his glass and then filled mine. It was like being back on the nightside when I was a kid, interviewing the father of the slain gang leader. They never really knew what happened, and the reporter was just the guy who came around to look at what was left of their busted lives. But the $42,000,000 was real. So was Pepe Fuentes. And so was Annie Fletcher, out on the Brooklyn Bridge with her broken neck.

"Did Pepe have an office here?"

"Down the hall."

"Can I take a look?"

"Why not?"

Pepe's office was a smaller version of Caldwell's, carved out of a couple of murdered oak trees. On the walls there were pictures of the same man who was sitting in the sun with Annie in the picture over in Brooklyn. Only Annie wasn't on the wall. The Pope was. Golda Meir was. And so were Cardinal Cooke and Eugene McCarthy and a couple of Secretaries of the Treasury. There was even a younger, leaner Pepe Fuentes, without a moustache, standing beside the late Cardinal Spellman.

"Looks like with half an effort, this guy could have taken off with St. Patrick's Cathedral."

"Possibly."

"Too bad you don't have windows up here. We could look outside and check whether it's still there."

"Maybe that's who did him in," Caldwell said, "the man upstairs."

"God? Nah. He doesn't have hitmen anymore."

"That sounds like blasphemy, Briscoe. Are you a Catholic?"

"My mother was."

I started opening drawers in the oversized desk. They were all empty.

"They cleaned it out this morning," Caldwell said. "Everybody was here. The F.B.I., the banking commission people, the IRS, the U.S. Attorney's office. I don't think they got much."

I looked at the area outside the office. There was a small desk beside the door, with a multi-button phone on top. I opened the top drawer. It was clean too.

"Anne Fletcher work here?"

He looked surprised again. "Why, yes."

I played dumb. "She come in today?"

"No. She . . . well, we heard from the police this morning that . . . well, she was killed last night in a car crash."

"Killed? Really? Jesus, this is a tough place to work, isn't it?"

"That isn't very funny, Mister Briscoe."

"No it isn't. I'm sorry. I'm just doing my Hildy Johnson act."

He stood there, leaning against the frame of the door. Somewhere a phone was ringing. He looked forlorn.

"I understand now why they don't have windows in these offices," I said.

"That wouldn't do me any good," Caldwell said.

"No. I guess it wouldn't."

"Well," he said. "Merry Christmas."

"Same to you," I said, but I didn't really mean it.

7

I walked up to the Olympic Towers to see the widow, but the uniformed gunsel at the door told me that Mrs. Fuentes had left town. He didn't know when. He didn't know with whom. He didn't know what she looked like. He didn't know about kids. He just knew what he was told. I slipped him a pound and he told me that Mrs. Fuentes was a blonde, good-looking, well-built, and she'd left two days ago. He didn't remember about the kids. I slipped him another pound and he told me the kids had left with the grandfather three weeks before the wife. The grandfather was a cranky old bastard who didn't speak English too good. The blonde wife looked scared when she left. Mister Fuentes was in and out a lot, and sometimes he'd take hookers upstairs, even with the wife there. The wife left with an American guy, and they had a lot of luggage. Just a regular-looking American. Big, regular-looking. The apartment was closed up tight. I didn't think he had five dollars' worth of anything left in him, so I slipped into a phone booth beside Scribner's and called Charlie Kelly at Homicide. Someone asked me to hold, and I watched the girls walking by on the wet streets for a long time, and dropped in thirty-five cents in extra nickels. Then a voice came back and told me that Charlie Kelly wasn't in and they didn't know when he would be back. I hung up. The only thing I could be sure about was that St. Patrick's Cathedral was still there.

I walked up Fifth Avenue to 57th Street, looking at the expensive trinkets of the rich that were piled in the windows. A fake Santa Claus stood on every corner, hustling for quarters, and there was a mob in front of F. A. O. Schwarz, looking at the toys. The main avenues were clear of snow now but the side streets were still piled up.

I remembered one Christmas when Anne and I had jumped into the car and driven all the way to the end of Long Island, and holed up for three days in Gurney's Inn at Montauk. The beach was empty, spotted with frozen mounds of snow. The wind drove lovely patterns into the sand, and we woke in the mornings with stalactites of ice hanging from the windows, and argued about the difference between stalactites and stalagmites. In the afternoon we argued about Kafka. We ended every argument in bed. She had the most flawless skin I'd ever known.

But there would be no Christmas for her now. She was dead. And now I was reasonably certain she had been murdered. She had been in a panic, coming to see me with papers. The papers must have been about the bank. About a $42,000,000 killing. And someone did not want those papers to be seen by a reporter, no matter how broken-down and retired. The someone could have been Pepe Fuentes except that he happened to be dead at the time. But Anne Fleacher might not have been the only person murdered over $42,000,000. It sounded as if Pepe Fuentes could have been killed in the sky over Mexico. I went into the Plaza, and found a pay phone. I called Frank Martin at Technology House, the palace of foundation grant money that made him respectable to the world. Frank the Fixer. Frank, who had brought Pepe Fuentes around to meet the marks.

Frank Martin was out of the country.

Beautiful.

Anne Fletcher was dead.

Pepe Fuentes was dead.

Pepe's wife was out of the country.

His rabbi Frankie the Fixer was out of the country.

The cop on the case was out of the office.

The $42 million was out of the bank.

It was as if the whole world was on hold. I left the Plaza and went back down to 57th Street and started crosstown for the Henry Hudson Hotel. An hour in the gym would straighten my brain. Right. Hit the heavy bag a couple of rounds. Lift some weights. Run around the track a few laps. Sit in the sauna. Burn off the fatigue. Perfect.

I was crossing Sixth Avenue when I first picked up the tail, reflected in the window of a Brew and Burger.

He was a six-footer with a plaid hat, a raincoat, and large feet. I slipped easily around a fat woman and he slipped around her a little too quickly, keeping the rulebook eighteen feet behind me. I stopped to look in the window of a piano store, and he stopped to look in the window of a Greek restaurant. I slowed my walk, and he slowed his. I hurried along a little faster and he hurried along a little faster.

At the Art Students' League I looked up at the paintings in the windows and then went in. The lobby was full of bearded young men and ivory-skinned girls with long dark hair tied in pony tails, and dark sweaters and dirty sneakers. The place smelled of turpentine and varnish. I went over and looked at the bulletin board for a while and then went into the cashier's office and asked for a catalogue.

When I went outside again, the spook was looking in the window of a health food store near the corner.

I jaywalked across the street and walked along the other side. I crossed Seventh Avenue and then Eighth. Up ahead was a little bar that Willie Pep used to front after he lost the championship to Saddler. It had a new name now. I bought a *Post* at the newsstand and took it with me into the bar.

The place was low and dark. A balding guy with jittery eyes was tending bar. A heavy blonde sat near the door, soaked in perfume. On the jukebox, Sinatra was singing about how Saturday night was the loneliest night of the week. They had bars like this in every big city in America and Sinatra was singing in all of them. I put a twenty on the bar, ordered a vodka on the rocks, and turned over the *Post* to the sports section. Vic Ziegel had a nice piece about Joe Frazier, who was talking about fighting again, but the rest of it was football gibberish. There was a long piece about a dull movie. I ordered another drink. The bartender took two dollars from my mound of change. The blonde lady got up and stuffed a dollar's worth of quarters into the jukebox and punched some buttons. Sinatra started to sing again. "In the Wee Small Hours of the Morning." It was still daylight outside.

"Boy, he is still the chairman of the board," she said.

"Chairman of the broads, you mean," the bartender said.

She laughed dirtily. "He's the best."

"Nobody ever touched him," the bartender said. "He is still the king."

"He's better than he ever was."

"They all came and gone. That Vic Damone. A while there I thought he was gonna do it all. But he went too. They all came and gone."

"Frank is still the chairman of the board," the blonde said.

The tail finally came in the door. I didn't look up. I couldn't hear his voice over the sound of Sinatra, but the bartender brought him a Dewar's and soda. He gave the bartender a five, and when the change came back, he picked it up and put it in his pocket. So I knew he wasn't from New York. I tried to read Max Lerner. The second paragraph made me realize that I'd only had four hours sleep.

Then I folded the *Post* over and left it beside my change on the bar and walked down through the back and into the men's room. And I waited. Two minutes. Five minutes. Seven minutes. I knew he couldn't stand it for too long. His head would be full of back doors and open windows leading into alleys. And he would have to fill out a report to his bosses

—whoever they were—and if he lost me, he would look like a putz. Eight minutes.

The door opened.

I saw his face, grabbed his tie and yanked him inside. I hit him in the neck with the free hand and when his hands came up, I reached in and yanked a .38 police special from under his armpit. I jammed the tip of the gun barrel into one of his nostrils. With the other hand I looked for a wallet. He didn't have one. They never do.

"All right, prick, who are you?"

He said: "You better take that gun away."

"I might take it away smoking, pal."

His eyes were more wan now. "Put it down. Please."

"Fuck you."

"You're in a lot of trouble, Briscoe. Right now you are in a lot of trouble."

"Not as much as you are, fatso. I just might blow your fucking head off."

I shoved the tip of the barrel into his nostril, spreading the cartilage, and then took off the safety.

"You're fooling around with the United States Government."

"Yeah? What outfit? C.I.A.? F.B.I.? I.R.S.? Do I owe you money or something? Where's your ID, buster? Tattooed on your ass?"

I could hear the bartender coming before I could see him. I backed away, with the pistol still pointed at the guy's bridgework, put my shoulder against the door and pushed out. The bartender was right there.

"All right, let's get it straight! We don't allow no fags in this pl . . ."

He stared at the pistol in my hand, and the other guy's red-nosed face.

"I'm glad you're here," I said. "I've been after this bum for days. He's been copping joints in men's rooms all over town."

"That's bullshit, I—"

"Shut up, scumbag," I said.

I handed the bartender the gun.

"Keep this degenerate covered. I'm going for a car."

"Right."

He had the pistol trained on the spook as I walked out. Sinatra was singing about Nancy with the laughing face. The heavy blonde did not smell as good as she thought she did.

8

I found a cab on Ninth Avenue and went downtown to Lexington and 55th. Then I walked the last block over to Clarke's to wait for Charlie Kelly. I sat at one of the small round tables next to the back door and had a beer. A kid came in selling papers. I took a late *Post*. There was nothing about a $42,000,000 killing.

The bar started to fill up with downtown types in tweed vests and faces. I ordered another beer and went over to the pay phone and called my service.

Nora Ephron had called from *Esquire* looking for the article I owed them now for two weeks. Someone had called from the Diner's Club about my bill. Moya Vargas had called.

"What time was that?" I asked.

"At, let's see, three-forty, Mr. Briscoe. She said it was urgent. She said she was at the airport and she was leaving town."

"Urgent, huh? She didn't say anything else?"

"Just that it was urgent."

I stepped out of the pay phone and went back to my table. The bar was very full now. I looked at the *Post* again. Not a whisper of the $42,000,000 plundering of the bank. It was Thursday. They would probably wait to make the announcement until after the stock market closed on Friday.

Urgent. If Moya had something to tell me, and it was really urgent, then she would have waited until she found me. But she had left town.

I looked up from the paper and saw Danny Lavezzo coming in the side door. He owns Clarke's.

49

He has a sly, sad face and the kind of eyes that come from hanging around a lot of places late at night. I waved him over. He took off his coat and sat down.

"What's doin'?" he said.

"I'm working on a story, Danny. About a guy named Pepe Fuentes."

"That son of a bitch."

"You know him?"

"He ran up a tab here."

"Large?"

"Very. He came in one night with a party of twelve, and didn't have cash or a check."

"Were you dunning him?"

"I sent him three bills. Over to that bank. I never got an answer. A deadbeat. One of those Latin-American deadbeats that come into town every once and a while."

"How come you gave him a tab?"

"His friends. He came in with a lot of people I knew. Regulars. People with some kind of class."

"Did he ever come in with Anne Fletcher?"

Danny looked at me with those sad nightside eyes. "Yeah. A couple of times."

"Alone?"

"Once alone. Once with a party."

He waved at a bartender and made a pouring gesture with his thumb. Then: "What's this all about?"

"I'm not sure yet, Danny. I'm just not sure."

I went to the phone and dialed Moya Vargas. Just in case she'd missed her plane. The phone rang nine times and nobody answered. When I went back to the table, Danny was sipping a black coffee and looking at the race results in the back of the paper. There was a shot of brandy beside the coffee cup.

"You know a girl named Moya Vargas?"

Lavezzo laughed. "Who you doing this story for? *El Diario?*"

"She's about five eight, good body, tan skin, black

hair pulled back tightly, high cheekbones. A slight accent."

His face started to change, as if he remembered something.

"She a hooker?" he said.

"Could be. But maybe not."

"Want me to ask someone?"

"Yeah."

"Hold it a minute."

He went into the pay phone and closed the door. I glanced through the paper. People were killing each other in Lebanon, Northern Ireland and Rhodesia. Four kids had burned to death out in Bed-Stuy, because the fire engine was putting out a fire somewhere else. A known gambler was found with two in the ear out in Sheepshead Bay. But there was nothing about Anne Fletcher being killed in the snow. Nothing about Pepe Fuentes exploding over the mountains of Mexico. And there was nothing at all about a guy who had followed me across 57th Street with a gun parked in his armpit.

Lavezzo came back.

"A broad named Moya Vargas was a hooker for a while," he said. "Showed up in town about a year, year and a half ago. Call girl. Very high-priced. Worked out of an apartment on the East Side. Then just dropped out of the racket. My guy says everybody figured she just made a big score with some john and retired."

"She a Mexican?"

"Funny you ask," Lavezzo said. "My guy said she was from Switzerland. Even though she used that Latin name, she had a Swiss passport."

"How would he know what kind of passport she carried?"

"I don't know. Probably got her some job in the Bahamas or something. He mentioned it. I didn't."

He threw down the brandy, sipped the coffee and got up.

"Thanks, Danny."

"I'll see you later. I gotta go back and whip the help."

He went into the back room. I called a waiter over and ordered two hamburgers and the spinach salad. While I was eating the first hamburger, Charlie Kelly came in. He looked tired. I waved to the empty chair.

"Hello, Charlie."

"You need a shave, Briscoe."

"I need a good night's sleep too. Want something to eat?"

"You buying?"

"If it's hamburger, I'm buying. If it's steak, you're buying."

"Hey, Jimmy. Two burgers medium and a salad."

I started on the second burger. "How's business?"

"Booming. We're averaging four point seven homicides a day this year."

"What's point seven of a homicide?"

"It's like point seven of a pregnancy."

I finished the burger as his salad arrived. "Moya Vargas skipped town, Charlie."

His eyes looked interested but he was working on the salad, holding a slice of tomato almost daintily between his fingers. He bit into the tomato.

"I don't blame her," he said. "There's days I feel like skipping town myself. In fact, I feel that way almost every day."

"Did you put a tail on me today, Charlie?"

"What?"

"I asked you whether you put a guy on me today?"

He laughed. "You've got to be kidding. You're not important enough to be tailed, Briscoe."

"That's what I thought. But someone was on me today."

"Really?"

"I think he was a *Federale*. Big, with a thirty-eight under his arm. No wallet I could find."

"Why a *Federale*?"

"Dumb."

"The Feds really believe in hiring the handicapped, that's for sure."

"I took his gun off him in the men's room."

Kelly laughed. The waiter put down his burgers. "Now I *know* he must have been a Fed. If you could take a gun off him, it's certain." He took a greedy bite of his first burger. "What did you do with the gun?"

I told him. He laughed again. "No shit? Jesus, that's beautiful."

"I'd like to find out where this Moya Vargas went, Charlie."

"Why?"

"I think she can tell me why Anne Fletcher was killed."

His face was sober now. "We're carrying that as an accident, Sam. I know how you felt about her, but it looks like an accident."

"Take a gander at the left rear fender."

"I did."

"It looks to me like someone sideswiped her, Charlie."

He stopped eating. There was still something in his mouth, but he was chewing it drily now.

"I thought about that," he said. "But it didn't make any sense. There are a lot of other ways to kill someone in this town. How the hell does a guy know that the bridge will be empty? That it will be snowing? That he can be sure she dies? It's just too sloppy for murder." He gave me a sad look. "I'm sorry to talk this way, Sam, but . . ."

"She's getting buried tomorrow," I said. "Can you have the coroner look at her once more?"

"Sure."

The waiter took his plate. He ordered a brandy and water and a coffee.

"Whatever happened to you and her anyway?" he said.

"I was never sure. I came home one day and she was gone."

"Damn."

"The worst thing was the books. She took all her books out of my bookshelves. It looked like a mouth with half the teeth knocked out. But that's how I knew she was gone for good."

"It's that goddamned women's lib. They all want to be free, or something."

"It might just have been me, Charlie. I'm no bargain."

"That why you quit the paper that time?"

"You're not as dumb as you look, Charlie."

"If I was," he said, "I'd go to work for the Feds." He sipped the brandy.

"Do me a favor, Charlie."

"If it don't cost me money."

"Have someone check the airlines and see where this Moya Vargas went. She's traveling on a Swiss passport, so it shouldn't be too hard."

"A *Swiss* passport?"

"She's not exactly your average-looking wetback, Charlie."

"And she uses the name Vargas."

"Apparently. Try the lines to Mexico City."

He went to the pay phone. Some of the tweed faces were beginning to stagger. It was dark out and snow was falling again. I looked at Kelly in the phone booth, and he was dialing a second number. Lavezzo came out of the back room with his overcoat on, nodded good night and went out the side door. Ben Gazzara came in with a couple of guys. They all had snow on the shoulders of their overcoats, and they moved into the back room. I was thinking about what a fine actor Gazzara was, and how I wished he would come back and do a play on Broadway, when Kelly came over and sat down.

"She left for Mexico this afternoon. Aeronaves flight one oh seven, out of Kennedy."

I put a twenty on the table and slipped the waiter a five.

"Where you going?"

"Sleighriding," I said.

"Be careful," Kelly said. "Bellywhopping hurts."

9

I fell asleep in the tub, soaking in hot water and Badidas, and dreamed obscurely of pistols and the dry high mesas of Mexico. Moustached men moved in the shadows of mountains. A body lay like a bag of laundry at the foot of a giant cactus. Then I was in a cell, the windows barred, and men were sitting against the wall staring at me. One of them made a move for my necktie. I moved away, afraid, ready to fight. And woke up.

I knew then that I was going to Mexico. Pepe Fuentes had died in Mexico. His father was in Mexico. His wife was in Mexico. Moya Vargas was in Mexico. It was none of my business, I suppose. I wasn't a cop. And the $42,000,000 wasn't mine. If anything, my instinct is to cheer when people stick up banks. But Anne Fletcher was my business, a long time ago. She was on her way to see me when she died. In the morning, she was going to be buried in the iron earth of a cemetery out in Queens. I felt I owed it to her to find out why she died.

I got out of the bath and dried off with a large rough towel and brushed my teeth until my gums hurt. I went over to the phonograph and put the Miles Davis "Spanish Blood" album on the turntable. I took *Tristram Shandy* out of the bookcase and carried him up the ladder to the sleeping bay. The cold of the new storm seeped into the loft. I turned on the electric blanket and slid under the covers. The bed seemed very large and very empty. For the first time in weeks, I wished I had a woman beside me.

I woke up at a little after three.

Someone was on the roof.

57

The sleeping bay was dark, and tucked back out of sight of anyone who tried to look through the skylight. I lay there, very still, and listened again. The footsteps moved. Stopped. Then moved again. It could be a junkie, but the junkies usually didn't work in bad weather. They waited for the summer, when a man could move fast up an alley with a TV set under his arm and make the quick moves if the cops showed. On a bad night in the snowiest winter in years, the man on the roof wasn't a junkie.

It had to be one of the Feds.

If he was a Fed.

If he didn't work for any of a number of outfits that might want to lean on me a little. I reached into the night table drawer and took out the .38.

The gun was cold in my hand. Years before, doing an article about the education of cops, I heard a teacher at the Police Academy explain to his class that cops used a .38, instead of a smaller caliber pistol, because it killed better. As I pulled on pants, boots and a ski jacket, I hoped I wouldn't have to kill anyone.

Someone was scraping snow off the skylight now. I waited.

From the darkness of the sleeping bay I could see the skylight, but the guy on the outside couldn't see me. The snow scraped off quickly, but there was a layer of mottled ice covering the glass. A knife started chipping the ice away.

Then I saw the face.

El putzo from 57th Street.

And in the reflected light of the living room lamp, I could see his eyes searching the dark areas of the loft. Fresh snowflakes melted on the scraped glass. He could see the silver strip of the alarm system. Then his face disappeared. I could hear his big feet clomping over the roof. He was heading for the stairway housing. I hurried down the ladder. If he was going to break into the apartment, I was going to help him. My door is steel-lined with a steel frame.

It has a double Fox lock and a steel bar holding the door in place. You would need an acetylene torch to get in.

But I wanted to make it easy.

While he worked the rooftop door, I lifted the bar, and removed the Fox lock, and stood to the side.

I heard him come down the stairs. He was moving softly, but the stairs were sixty years old, and each time he moved he squeaked.

He reached the landing in front of my door. It took him a while, but he got the two locks open. He tried the handle. It turned. He pushed the door in an inch. Then a few more inches. Then shoved it wide.

And I skulled him with the gun butt.

He fell away, making a gurgling sound. I kicked him behind the ear, and then socked him again with the gun.

He lay flat out on his back.

I took his gun and put it in the bathroom, and then I stripped him to his shorts. There wasn't a label in the coat or the shirt, not a piece of identification. I went to the garage area where I kept Red Emma, and found three extension cords and tied his arms and legs. He was a big bastard. More than six feet, about 220 pounds, running to fat. A thin bubble of blood was forming in his mouth. I took his pulse. He was all right, but he was going to have a headache.

I lugged him down the hall and opened the trunk of Red Emma. Chamaco was off for the night, so I used the key to call the elevator. I braced his shoulders against the bumper and heaved. His body made a large soft A, before crumpling sideways into the trunk. I threw his clothes in on top of him and locked the trunk. I put his gun in the front seat.

Then I went out in the hall and up the flight of squeaky steps and closed the roof door. I went down again and locked my front door from inside. I got into Red Emma and drove her the six feet into the freight elevator, closed the steel safety doors behind me, and then went down to the street. My thoroughbred wasn't much car in the snow, but she was good enough for delivering a package.

I pulled up beside the Elizabeth Street station house. The street was empty. The snow fell steadily. I could see lights glowing thinly on the Brooklyn Bridge. There were no cops around, and no cars. I parked in the darkened area between streetlights and got out. I opened the trunk.

He was awake.

"What the hell are you doing?" he said.

"You're lucky I didn't blow your face off, buster."

I grabbed him roughly, and pulled his bound body toward me. He fell heavily into the gutter.

"Hey, you can't leave me here!"

"Shut up."

I threw his clothes on top of him, looked around, and went back to the car. He was struggling unsuccessfully to get to his knees, shivering in the snow, and looking forlorn. I got back out of the car again, holding his gun, and walked toward him, aiming the gun at his chest. His eyes widened in fear. I smiled. And then slid the gun into the sewer.

"You bastard, Briscoe! You son of a bitch!"

"Have a nice winter."

"I'll freeze to death, goddamn you!"

I stuffed his undershirt into his mouth.

"Bye."

Then I got back into Red Emma, drove to the Bowery and went right, moving fast down to Park Row, and around past City Hall. Traffic was completely dead now. At Broadway and Rector I jumped into a phone booth and called Elizabeth Street.

A cop picked up the phone. "Fifth precinct. Nolan."

"There's a degenerate outside in the snow," I said.

"Please state your name and phone number, sir."

"I said there is a pervert right outside your station house, Nolan. Balls-ass naked."

"Outside the station house?"

"Right out there in the snow. He eats undershirts."

"Hey, Charlie, is there . . . Hey, look at that maniac!"

I drove home, thinking that what I had done was probably illegal, knowing that I should have called the cops and had the guy booked for breaking and entering, and then called the city desk at the *News* or the AP and told them what had happened.

But I didn't have the time. Not for the cops. Not for the hours waiting at the station house while they checked with the guy's bosses in Washington or Foley Square. Not for the wait while the Feds worked the fix that would let him walk. I had seen too many of these government bastards over the years and I was too old to think that law-book justice could handle them. Your best and only hope was to rough them up in the dark before they got the chance to do it to you. It didn't matter which outfit they worked for. The Agency. The Bureau. The Company. They were always bigger than the law. Bigger than poor city cops chasing poor black felons around the streets of New York. They were even bigger than governments. And I didn't have the time for them. I was going somewhere in the morning. Going first to bury a girl. And then going to find out why so many people were suddenly dead, and why a nameless fat man was following me into men's rooms in dark daylight bars, walking across the rooftop of the place where I lived, moving into my life with a gun on his hip.

I was going to Mexico. The country where I once was young.

10

The skylight was covered with snow again when I got home. I dried off Red Emma with some old towels. Then I packed a bag, and threw a few books, a tape recorder, and a pile of tapes and batteries into the briefcase. I put bag and case at the door beside the Hermes 3000. I laid my passport on top of the typewriter. Then I went over to the fireplace, removed a brick on the side, and flicked the switch. The fireplace shifted on its rollers, opening like a door, and I went into the file room. I filed my gun under G because I'd never get it through airport security, and then took out the folder on Mexico. I copied some phone numbers into a notebook and put the folder back.

I went out, flicked the switch again and watched the fireplace roll into place. It was corny as hell, but the trick fireplace was one of the better investments I'd made with the money from Vegas. There were more files in two cabinets over near the window, but nothing worth stealing was in their folders. I knew that if anyone wanted to get into the fireplace and grab the other files they could do it. But my Irish carpenter had rigged alarms and sirens that made Maynard Ferguson sound as if he were blowing a Chiclet box. If they were going to rob me, it would have to be while I was out of town.

I went upstairs to the sleeping bay and set the alarm for ten.

I woke at nine, with a cold sun streaming into the loft through the skylight. The snow had melted. The panes were clear again. And it seemed strange to be going back to Mexico. For almost twenty years I had managed to fly over it, or around it, ducking it, avoiding it. I shaved, remembering myself with the beard I had then. Fidel and Che were already in the Sierra Maestra that year, wearing beards of their own, but mine was an artist's, not a revolutionary's. Revolution had never even occurred to me. That was the year when all I wanted was to be as good a painter as Jack Levine. Or Fletcher Martin. I loved looking at Kline and Motherwell and Pollock, who were the big New York painters that year, but I didn't want to paint like them. I was going to put human beings back in painting. I would learn rough painterly brush strokes from the abstract expressionists; I would steal their large bold designs. But I was going to have people in my paintings. Yeah. I was going to do a lot of things. And when Anne Fletcher died, she had a book about Fidel in her room, and a poster of Che, but there was no trace of me. I was the empty parenthesis.

I finished shaving and stepped into the shower. *Hace veinte años.* Twenty years ago. In Mexico. Where I was young.

I called the answering service and told them I would be in Chicago for a week. Then I put the bags on the freight elevator and pressed 4. I got off and rang Charlie Ginsberg's bell. Charlie really was a painter.

He answered the door, his bald head shining, his gray grizzled beard looking like aging Brillo.

"Are you crazy, Briscoe? You know what time it is?"

"I'm going out of town, Charlie."

I handed him the keys.

"Where to?"

"Alaska," I said. "Sleep upstairs if you can stand it. And be careful. There's some funny people looking for me."

"Again?"

"You know, sex-starved literary agents. Lunatic editors."

"And bad guys too?"

"Maybe."

He hefted the keys. "I'll bring the shotgun with me."

He meant it; Charlie had been wounded three times in Korea, and taken a few people with him while it was happening. One of them was a punk lieutenant from Arizona.

"If I get in trouble," I said, "I'll call the usual way."

"All right," he growled. "Watch your ass."

He looked behind him. A blowsy dark-haired girl sat up on the side of the mattress near the windows and lit a cigarette. She had a great body. All of Charlie's little girls did.

"Watch yours," I said, and got back on the elevator.

The cab from Scull's Angels pulled over to the side of the gravel path behind the hearse from Walter B. Cooke's. I told the driver to wait and moved across the snow to a little slope where Pete Jacobs was standing beside a fresh dark gash in the earth. He was wearing a Roman collar under the overcoat, but he was hatless, and thin wisps of hair blew in the wind. The people from Cooke's stood discreetly on the side. He nodded as I came over and we shook hands.

"Sorry I'm late."

"Don't worry about it," he said.

I looked down and saw the coffin, the dark wood glistening and wet. Some earth had already fallen across the brass plaque.

"You gave her a Mass?"

"Yes. I didn't think you'd want to come."

"No."

He squeezed my arm and then opened the prayer book. He started to say the words in English.

"Pete?"

"Yeah?"

"Do you remember it in Latin?"

"Of course."

He started again, this time in Latin. The new words had come in after she took her books out of my shelves, and I had never gotten used to them. I was still part of the old rituals, the obscurity of meaning, the mysteries of the dead language. In a way, the old words were like Anne Fletcher: dead now too, and full of ellipses. There were entire years of her life that were simply blanks now. Most of them were years before and after I knew her. That crazy time in Havana when Fidel and Che were cleaning up the mob's dirty little playground. Another time, after she dropped out of college for show business, when she spent her nights dancing around refrigerators at Miami Beach trade shows. There were years that other guys would remember, if I ever met them late at night. But the only years I knew about for sure were the few years she spent with me. I stared away, looking at the skyline, gray and majestic in the distance. There seemed to be an unbroken progression from the endless rows of crosses and markers to the granite spires of the skyscrapers across the river. I had a brief memory of the last painful months of my mother's life, and how she would call out at night for my dead father. Using the few words of Yiddish he had taught her. The words sounding like Gaelic. And how she would always say that the Celts were the lost tribe. The lost tribe of Israel, washed up on a green northern island. Calling for him. We were all the lost tribe. And then Jacobs was finished. He threw a symbolic handful of dirt on the coffin, and said one final prayer. I wished I could pray, but I had forgotten how. The wind tossed some loose snow into the oblong hole and it was over.

We walked back to the hearse together, while the gravediggers did their jobs.

"It's never easy, is it?" he said.

"No."

"I wish I could say something that would make it

more sensible. I don't have those words in me much anymore, Sam."

"Neither do I."

"She was a nice woman. The little I got to know her in those days."

"If you ask me whatever happened to us, I'll knock you down."

He smiled at me. "You don't punch hard enough for that."

I hugged him one final time and got into the cab and told the driver to hurry.

11

The departure lounge was filled with the usual assortment of people who come together at airports. Two young honeymooners, flushed and uncertain, sat glued together on a pair of plastic chairs. Businessmen, moving south to check their hired hands, read the *Times* or the *Wall Street Journal*, and had *US News and World Report*, *Time* and *Newsweek* on their laps. There were thirty middle-aged people traveling in a group, shouting and laughing and already half in the bag. I sat reading the *News* near the boarding entrance, glancing up from time to time to see if any of the other passengers were looking at me. One thing was sure: They wouldn't send my fat frozen friend around again. Even the Feds were not that dumb.

In the sports section Dick Young was defending the owners of baseball teams and in the front of the paper Suzy was doing her homework for the city's burglars, listing all the rich people who were wintering in Palm Beach. There were a lot of Christmas ads.

The flight was called and the tourist-class passengers started boarding first. I lit a cigarette and waited.

When I looked up a red-haired girl carrying a blue suitcase was rushing across the waiting room. She had on high heels and a tailored tweed suit and she was wearing large round Gloria Steinem glasses, tinted violet. Her legs were long, with turned out feet that told me she had once been a dancer. She talked rapidly to the Aeronaves clerk and handed him her passport and a credit card while he made out a ticket and told someone else to carry her bag on board. Her hair wasn't really red. It was the color of tangerines. She kept looking over her shoulder, while the clerk made out her tourist card. As I passed her on the way to an ashtray, I saw a scribble of fear run through her green eyes.

"Thank you, thank you," she said to the clerk in a husky voice. "Thank you."

And she rushed on board the plane, clutching her handbag and red first-class boarding pass.

I took one final look around the waiting room, didn't see any unfriendly faces, and decided it was time to board.

She was sitting in my seat.

A-1. Next to the window. Staring out at the mechanics, as they moved their blocks and forklifts and prepared for takeoff. The aisle seat was empty and every other seat in first class was full. I sat down beside her. I showed her my boarding card.

"Excuse me," I said. "But you're sitting in my seat."

My voice seemed to startle her. Her eyes shifted to the door. A stewardess was pulling various bars and levers, locking it from inside. Her face relaxed. She was about twenty-five.

"Oh, I'm sorry. I was in such a rush I didn't really . . ." She looked at her boarding pass. "We can shift right now if . . ."

"Forget it," I said. "This is fine. I'll just look past you when we go by the volcanoes."

"The volcanoes?" She had the husky voice of someone who had done a lot of hard singing or hard drinking.

"Popo and Ixtl," I said. "They're right outside Mexico City. Popocatepetl and Ixtlchihauatl. I forget what Popocatepetl means, but the other word means 'sleeping lady' in Aztec."

"You've been to Mexico City before?"

The plane was taxiing to its takeoff position now.

"A long time ago."

"I've never been," she said.

"It used to be a great town," I said, hating the edge of sentimentality that was creeping into my voice. "A friend of mine once wrote a book about the place called *Where the Air Is Clear*, and that's exactly what Mexico City was once. Clear and beautiful."

"It's got worse, huh?"

"Almost everything has," I said, and opened the briefcase and took out a copy of Cicero's murder trials and started to read. I could feel her eyes watching me, and I thought about those muscled dancer's legs, and then put her out of my mind. I was probably just too old for it; I had picked up too many people on too many airplanes in too many places, and it was fun when you were coming off a job and terrible when you were going on a job. And I was going on a job. The plane wound itself, the engines opening up, and then all 215 tons lifted at once, hurling us at the clouds. I read a few paragraphs about old and bloody crimes, and leaned back and slept.

I did not dream.

A stewardess woke me an hour later. I looked up and saw her smiling down at me, wet-lipped, with strong hawk-nosed Zapotec features, a downy moustache above those full red lips and hard white teeth, and a fleshy body under the uniform. She handed me a tray of snacks.

"Woo you like a drink, sir?"

"*Sí, señorita. Una cerveza, por favor.*"

She smiled even wider. "*Sí, señor.*"

I poked at the snack tray: some dried shrimps in a tepid sauce, calling itself *ceviche*, but blanded out for the tourist traffic. The redhead slept, her face falling, her breath coming thickly. Nerves twitched in her cheeks. Her hands moved in and out of fists. I did not envy her dreams.

The stewardess came back with a cold Bohemia, and smiled wetly again. As she walked forward, she shook a little more than she had the first time around the track.

I took off my jacket, folded it, put it in the over-head rack, and looked around at some of the others in the first class cabin: an elderly couple, dry as sand, heading for Ajijic or Lake Chapala, to live out the last thin years of retirement at a good exchange rate; one of those lean, tanned businessmen, a product of the Wharton School cookie cutter, reading the *Wall Street Journal* with the same absorption that his grandfa-ther's generation had reserved for the *Police Gazette;* a heavy-set Mexican man in a gray sharkskin suit, his face fleshy with years, his moustache trimmed to re-semble Arturo de Cordova's; a girl with bottle-yellow hair seated close beside him, holding his hand tightly.

The red-haired girl choked, sucked in air, and came suddenly awake.

She didn't seem to know where she was. She pulled away from me, and stared.

"Relax," I said.

"How long have I been asleep?" she murmured.

I looked at my watch. "Oh, an hour and a half. Didn't sleep much last night, huh?"

"No."

"Well, whatever it was, it's over now. You've split. There's no sense losing any more sleep over him."

"What makes you think you know what's going on in my life?"

"When someone's as scared as you are, it's usually about something that started out as love, and became something ugly."

"You've been there, I guess?"

"I've been everywhere, sweetheart."

The meal arrived: wilted lettuce, dry avocado, and watery tomato served on a soggy tortilla; bread-sticks; a chewy "New York" steak. Even the Seven-Up was flat. And while we ate, she talked. During meals on airplanes, people tell you the goddamnedest things. She started by telling me her name was Nick.

"Nick?"

"Nicola. I had a romantic mother. She saw the name in some Italian movie and gave it to me. My father started calling me Nick, because he wanted a son."

"Nice to meet you, Nick. My name's Shirley."

"Shirley?"

"Yeah. I had a romantic father."

She smiled, and I called for another *cerveza* for me and a bourbon for her. She started smoking a Benson and Hedges cigarette. The words flowed. The food didn't.

"What's his name?" I asked. "The guy you are now through with for life."

"Would you believe it? Lenny. And he's a comedian. At least he started out to be a comedian. He's not much of anything anymore. He stays home all day and lifts weights and then at night he gets dressed and goes out. He hits all the bars. He's really good-looking, you know? But he's the jealous type. You know, really nuts. He thinks I'm fooling around all the time and it just isn't true and there's nothing I can tell him to change his mind. If I went to midnight Mass, he'd figure I was doing the priest. And he has me crazy. Paranoid, you know? I mean he follows me around, he wants to go to my auditions, just so I don't ball anyone to get a job, which I would never do anyway, but he would never believe that, I guess because he's the type that *would* ball anyone if it meant getting a job. So about three weeks ago I got a job in a show in the Village, a good show, but a show where I had to, you know, take off my clothes and this drove him really around the bend. It was part of the play and very artistic but he hated it, hated it. Then one night he tried to beat me up. I couldn't believe it, he smacked me around and tied me up and left me there and then he went out, and I couldn't even get to a phone and call the theater and they went on without me and I couldn't even explain the next day to the producer. I mean, he didn't beat me

up, really, he just left me there, and then came in
that night with . . . with . . . with a hooker, and
while I was tied up, he . . ."

"Sounds like a wonderful guy."

"So finally I got fed up. I went to stay at my
girl friend's and for ten days I was all right. He didn't
know where to find me. I blew the job downtown,
and stopped going to the theater, you see, so he didn't
know *where* I was, but he was around somewhere.
And then one afternoon, when I showed up for an
audition for the new Fosse show, I saw him waiting
across the street in a doorway. He must have been
reading *Show Business* or one of the other trades, just
looking at the list of auditions, and I turned around
and left without going in, and he started to run after
me, right down Forty-seventh Street. I jumped in a
cab, and the cab got caught at a light, and he
punched the window—I locked the doors, see?—and
the cabbie went crazy, and got out with a wrench
or something, and a cop came over, and there was a
lot of blood, and he kept yelling that he was gonna
kill me. The cop took him away. That was yesterday.
I heard last night that they let him out, so I decided
to leave. Just get out of the country. Because I think
he would kill me. I do. I really do."

"Why did you marry this winner anyway?"

She smiled. "Because he made me laugh."

I laughed out loud and so did she. The parts of
her face that had fallen in sleep were back in their
proper places now.

"How old are you?" I said.

"None of your goddamned business."

"I knew you'd say that. I guess you know they
don't give quickie divorces in Mexico anymore."

She sipped the tepid coffee. Her voice, which had
risen an octave during her monologue, dropped down
again. "Who said I wanted a divorce?"

"You just want a little rest, huh?"

"Yeah. Maybe I can even get some work down
there."

"They're not too hot about giving unemployed *gringas* a break."

"They've got night clubs, don't they?"

"Well, they did when I was there. I suppose Acapulco has everything Miami has, plus enchiladas."

"Then I can always get a job."

"Suppose he comes after you?"

She looked at me, blinked, then looked away. The clouds drifted by. The captain said we were over Texas.

Then she turned to me again: "What's your racket, Sam?"

"I'm a writer."

Her face brightened. "Songs?"

"Everything else but."

"You write movies?"

"I have."

She had lost interest when she heard I didn't write songs and regained it when she heard I'd written movies. The glitter came into her eyes, and the bad husband and her bloody afternoon with the cabdriver vanished. You see that glitter in the eyes of politicians and movie stars and even an occasional editor, when some idea scurries across his brain in your presence. She was already casting herself in some movie I had not yet written. In some crazy way, she reminded me of Anne Fletcher: forever wanting something she couldn't have, and getting tangled up with a new Mister Wrong every other semester. She and Anne would have understood each other. And this damaged kid would have the same problems with me that Anne once had. They were part of the sisterhood of the hurt, these girls, and they needed a permanent audience of one. You were supposed to console, applaud, nurse, heal, and above all, listen. They never understood that when a writer looks out a window for an hour, he's working. The silence withers them. After a while, they go away, looking for an audience or a melodrama.

She fiddled with the airlines house organ in the

pouch before her. Then: "Are you working on a script now?"

"I don't write movies anymore."

Her eyes widened. "Really?" It was as if she could not imagine a world in which a writer would not write movies, given a choice. "Why not, for God's sake?"

"I couldn't stand the people," I said.

"Really?"

"Really."

She put out her cigarette in the tiny ashtray on the armrest. She had long coral-painted nails, but had chewed the sides of her fingers into a raw mess.

The stewardess took the trays away. I folded up the table, leaned back and closed my eyes. Nick hadn't told me her last name. But I hadn't told her mine either.

Mexico City was gone. It was down there all right, but I couldn't see it under the great fuming smear that filled the bowl made by the mountains. The smear was the color of dried pus.

Nick filled out her landing card, as I looked past her at the smear. Her last name was Carter. Nick Carter. I immediately thought better of her father.

We touched down on the tarmac with a bump, and she turned to me.

"I just realized something terrible. I don't have a hotel."

"Is this where I'm supposed to ask you to share mine?"

I smiled. She didn't.

"I didn't say that."

"You thought it."

She screwed her mouth around, biting something on the inside of her cheek.

"Yeah, I did."

I said, "You're a beautiful woman. I'd love to spend some time with you. I'd love to sleep with you. But I'm here on business."

"I understand," she said, very quietly. I said nothing. When a woman says that she understands, and the voice is very quiet, you know you have hurt her in some goddamned way. I didn't want to hurt her. There were people I wanted to hurt, and bad. But this poor kid, with her second-rate dreams, and poor crazy husband, wasn't one of them.

"Do you have money on you?" I said.

"Some."

"How much?"

"A couple of hundred."

"That should be enough for a couple of weeks, if you have credit cards."

She looked jittery now, as the plane taxied down the landing strip to the arrival area. "I have Bankamericard and Master Charge."

"American Express?"

"No."

"Well, it should be enough. How long are you staying?"

"Depends if I get work."

The plane stopped. Seatbelts clacked open. Arturo de Cordova had separated from his blonde girl friend and was sitting very stiffly, looking correct and remote. Briefcases came from under seats. I stood up, holding my briefcase. Nick Carter got up and smiled weakly.

"It was nice talking to you," I said. "Uh, if you need help, I'll be at the Hotel Geneva."

"Like the city in Sweden?"

"Switzerland."

Up close, she smelled like gardenias.

12

The cabdriver was very young and he drove carefully under the roof of poisoned air. The city had changed, but not as much as I had. We passed old men slathering concrete against walls, and facing them with brick, while young men peeled their shirts off under a fine thin rain and whistled loudly at the women in the passing cars. Posters from old elections peeled off the walls, and the driver said that it was very hard now in Mexico, the inflation was very hard, the devaluation was very hard. Except for the rich, I said. And he said that it was never very hard for the rich, anywhere in the world.

I laughed and he asked me if I knew Mexico. And I said, yes, I knew Mexico. Twenty years ago, I said, I was a student here. The driver said that he too was a student, but everything had been different twenty years ago. How did he know? His grandfather had told him.

So I did not ask him whether he had ever seen Toluco Lopez boxing at the Arena Mexico in the year when he was the best fighter on the earth. I did not ask about Pajarito Moreno either, who had knocked out all the Americans when they came down to fight at 7,300 feet above sea level, and was destroyed when he went to fight them at sea level in Los Angeles. I didn't ask whether the woman named Pechos de Oro still worked at the Tupinamba Club on Calle Niño Perdido, and I didn't tell the boy about what happened to me on the night of the Feast of the Immaculate Conception, when I started for a whorehouse and ended in the Lecumberri Prison.

I just sat there, as he moved through the light rain,
taking the side streets, heading for the Zona Rosa.

He had seemed surprised when I told him I
wanted the Hotel Geneva, and I knew then that the
hotel must no longer be what it had been. But once,
when I was his age, I had seen Fletcher Martin walking on the Reforma at dusk with a thin and elegant
blonde woman, and he had looked exactly like what I
thought a painter should be: big-chested, with slop-
ing fighter's shoulders, a hand-worked nose, and fierce
Zapata moustaches. I had followed him into the Zona
Rosa, past the art galleries and the trinket shops, and
he had gone into the Hotel Geneva. He looked happy
that day and I always thought that the hotel had as
much to do with it as the blonde. So I had chosen the
Geneva, whether or not it had seen better days. Everything else had too.

It wasn't really as bad as I had expected. The
driver double-parked his cab and helped me out with
my bag. I over-tipped him, of course, adding further
to the inflation of the peso. A doorman smiled me into
the lobby. At the front desk a gruff older man handed
me the registration blank and asked for my passport.
I looked down the hall, and saw that the lights were
out in the great high-ceilinged gallery. Middle-aged
bellboys were hanging around, and the cigar store
was full of older tourists buying postcards and silver
junk.

"*Está solo?*" the man said.

"*Sí, señor.*"

Of course I was alone. Did he think I was carrying a midget in the suitcase? *Bueno.* He shrugged,
called to a bellman, and handed me a heavy brass
key.

There were two narrow single beds in the room,
a varnished night table with a Cinzano ashtray sitting
on a doily, a large closet, a card table with a standing
lamp beside it, and a huge eight-drawer bureau.

I over-tipped the bellboy too.

He went out and I unpacked. There were wire

hangers in the closet, left over from old laundry. I hung everything up, and then went to the window. A print curtain covered old-fashioned venetian blinds with thick slats. I peeked through the slats. I could see over the roof of the gallery, and out toward the neon glow of Insurgentes. The giant caped figure of the man who sold brandy loomed behind a Pepsi-Cola sign. He looked forlorn. And oddly familiar. I had already met Nick Carter; maybe the sign was a warning that I was also going to meet the Shadow.

I went in and shaved again, and showered and lay down on the bed with a towel across my middle and tried to think.

I was in Mexico. I was looking for someone in the family of Pepe Fuentes, because maybe someone in the family of Pepe Fuentes would tell me why Anne Fletcher was murdered. Maybe someone would tell me where Judge Crater was too. It was ridiculous. Even if they knew, they had no reason to tell me. But there was more to this than I knew. It was about the looting of a New York bank, at least one killing, a death in a plane crash, and maybe the C.I.A. too. And it was my arrogant reporter's pride that I might somehow be able to unravel it. I had to find Moya Vargas too, and I was certain that the Fuentes family knew where she was. She had lied to me by leaving out a lot of the details. This time I would get the details. I would cut through her glib performance and make her tell me what really happened to Anne Fletcher in the final weeks of her life.

I was thinking these things, in the dim room, when I fell asleep.

The phone woke me a few minutes after eleven. I wasn't expecting anyone.

I let it ring.

Six. Seven. Eight rings.

It stopped.

I thought about my fat friend sitting in his shorts in the snow on Elizabeth Street.

The phone rang again.

I wished I had a gun.

I let it ring nine times, while I dressed.

It rang for the third time while I was slipping out the door.

My room was on the second floor. I waited briefly at the end of the hall, next to a fire door, but I didn't hear anyone coming. I ignored the elevator and walked down the marble steps of the main staircase to the lobby.

The cigar store was closed and so was almost every other shop. I felt itchy. Probably from dust in the room. Or the Mexican water. Or the cheap soap. I went to the desk and left my key with the same man who had checked me in.

"Are there any messages?" I asked him in Spanish.

He glanced at the boxes. *"No, señor."*

"But someone rang my room."

"And you didn't speak to them?"

"No."

He gave me that all-purpose Yankees-Are-Crazy shrug. "In that case . . ."

"A favor. Don't give anyone my room number, all right?"

"Sí, señor."

"One more thing."

"Sí, señor."

"Has Miss Carter registered yet?"

He looked at something on the wall out of my line of sight.

"Carter?"

I spelled it for him, and gave it a more pronounced Spanish pronunciation. Car-tair.

"No, señor."

"Bueno. Muchissimas gracias."

A thin rain was still falling. It was the wrong season for rain. The summer was the time of rain. All the guidebooks said so. The guidebooks tell you a lot of things.

I walked to the corner of Calle Londres where a pimp promised me a good time, then I turned left along a street of curio shops jammed with cheap junk. Rock and roll was blasting from the lounge of the Intercontinental Hotel. I turned right on Liverpool, trying to remember where everything was. The streets were very crowded. Women with sick, dirty children were begging from every other doorway. Young pasty-faced children of the upper class crawled along in American cars. The sidewalks were cracked and broken. The streets were dirtier. When I was young, there were four million people in the city. Now I could feel the force of a full thirteen million pushing in, driving to the center, eating, drinking, shitting, dying, fornicating and killing. There was a new kind of tension in the air, something that could implode into revolution. Newsboys seemed more desperate, the pimps more aggressive, the hookers more blatant, as they all chased the last *chavo* of the night. Loose change. Make a buck. You like pretty girl? Very lot of fun, *señor. Un peso. Un peso. Señor. Un peso. Un poco de chavo. Señor. Un peso.*

Sanborn's was still lit, but the streets around it were darker. The energy crisis had hit Mexico too, and as I bought some newspapers, I realized that none of the cities in which I had been young would ever look dazzling and gorgeous again at night. They needed the oil for the factories, and the big stores, and the government buildings and the jails, not for wasted enchantments. We would live in the darkened cities at night, all of us reduced to citizens of some Albanian backwater, dreaming of the bright past.

I bought *Esto* and *Ovaciones*, the sports papers, and picked up *Siempre*, a couple of crime weeklies, and *Excelsior*, the great plump semi-official newspaper. I looked at the headlines in *Excelsior* as I walked through Sanborn's to the restaurant area in the back. At the foreign newsstand, the *Times* was a day old, but I bought a copy of the *News*, the city's English-language newspaper.

The restaurant was only a quarter full. A group of eight or nine young men sat together at three joined tables, looking around at the few scattered young women, who sat in the icy possession of mothers or grandmothers. I started to read *Esto*. The faces of the fighters were all new, but the stories were the same. So-and-So trained yesterday at the Baños Jordan for his big fight at the Arena Mexico on Saturday night, and was applauded by hundreds of fans as he left. So-and-So had been offered so many pesos to fight Such-and-Such in Los Angeles, but his manager said that he had other obligations. This generally meant that the manager of so-and-so thought his fighter would get flattened by such-and-such and didn't want anything to do with him, especially if he could book his tiger with an unemployed cigar salesman in a main event in Leon.

"*Buenas noches, señor.*"

I looked up and a waitress in a Tehuantepec costume was standing before me, holding a giant menu. She had a thick, short-legged Indian body and an absolutely dazzling smile.

"*Buenas noches, señorita.*"

"*Quiere café?*" she said.

"*Como no.*"

She left the menu and went away for a while and got a coffeepot and came back and poured it for me and gave me that smile again and waited with her pad and pencil. I ordered *enchiladas suizas* and some bottled water. She smiled and went away again.

I was scanning the day-old wire service copy in the *News* when I found Pepe Romero's column. This is a gossip column in the old style, full of three-dot items recording the comings and goings of people you don't really care about, told in souped-up language that sounds like Winchell without the malice.

Halfway down the column, I saw the item:

"*At the Chalet Suizo, bumped into Moya Vargas, stunning ex of late Pepe Fuentes. Sorry she missed*

*the burial services, says the beauteous Moya, but she
received word too late . . ."*

That was all.

I read it again.

And then stared at it, as if the two sentences
would step off the page, and explain themselves.

Explain why Moya Vargas never mentioned that
first marriage when she told me about Pepe Fuentes.
Explain what Moya Vargas was really doing with
Anne Fletcher, who had been sleeping with her ex-
husband. Explain why Moya Vargas, the New York
call girl, the secret ex-wife, the friend of a girl I used
to love, had hurried down to Mexico, leaving behind
snow and a corpse. Explain why she had left a message saying she was leaving, playing slick spider to
my slow fly.

"Sus enchiladas, señor."

The waitress gave me that smile, and put the
enchiladas with green sauce in front of me. She
opened the bottled water and walked away. I decided that she wasn't flirting. She just liked to
smile.

I ate quickly and went to the pay phone and
called the *News*. Romero wasn't in the office. He
wasn't even at home. He was in Los Angeles and
would be back in a week. I thanked the bored telephone operator and went back to the booth. The waitress smiled her thanks as I paid the check, and wished
me a good night.

13

It was after midnight. The rain had stopped. I looked at my list of addresses and phone numbers, and walked along Calle Liverpool past the Galeria Misrachi and the shuttered restaurants to the Reforma. The great plane trees rose to the sky. But the old paths of hard-packed earth had been replaced by tezontle stone, and the old one-peso cabs, which for a single peso took you anywhere on a straight line along the Reforma, had become three-peso cabs. The cars were bigger, the pollution denser, but I still saw servant girls drifting down from the huge gloomy houses of the rich to meet their young men under the trees. I still smelled the old Mexico City smell, which, once you have smelled it, you can never forget: a smell made from carbon fires on rooftops, azalea trees blooming in hidden gardens, burnt petroleum, a million tortillas frying on open stoves, all of them refined and mixed by the high thin air. That was Mexico, and it was still the same.

But when I turned into Bucareli Street, the old cigar store where I would buy the brown-papered cigarettes called Negritoes was gone. So was the *Dia y Noche* cantina. An office building stood on that corner now, and traffic choked the avenue. I walked down Bucareli to the offices of *Novedades*, which was the best newspaper in the country. The Universal Press office was on the sixth floor. A guard asked for identification. I showed him a New York working press card, which looked very official, and told him in Spanish that I had just arrived from Washington. He nodded grimly and let me into the elevator.

A bearded young American and a flat-faced Mexican man in his forties were the only people in the office. The Mexican was punching copy on a telegraph machine. The American was sitting with his feet up on a desk, drinking coffee and reading the *Village Voice*. He looked up when I came in and went back to reading the paper without saying a word. The paper was three weeks old.

"Hiya doin'?" I said.

"Hi."

"I'm a reporter, in town on a story. Can I use your files? I want to look at some clips."

He looked around the side of the paper, his brow furrowing.

"You're a reporter?"

"No, I'm actually here selling nuclear reactors. I thought that reporter bit would soften you up."

He put the paper down and slowly stood up. He was tall and gangly, with a pair of ragged dungarees, Frye boots, and a thick Oaxaca sweater over a T-shirt bearing a portrait of Marilyn Monroe. He was very young so I forgave him everything except Marilyn; he hadn't earned the right to that nostalgia; Marilyn belonged to my generation.

"You do comedy, huh?"

"Only in bed," I said.

He came around the desk and looked as if he wanted to smile but couldn't permit himself the luxury. I handed him the press card and said: "How about a half a dollar for a fellow American?"

He looked at my name, and then at my face.

"You're Sam Briscoe?"

"I don't have to show you no steenking badges, Meester Dobbs."

He smiled. "I've been reading you since I was a little kid."

"Everybody has. What about those clips?"

The kid stuck out his hand and I shook it. "I mean it. I've been reading your column all my life."

"I don't write the column anymore."

"Really? Jesus, I've been away too long."

"What's your name again?"

He shrugged. "Murray Peters. You never heard of me."

"Are you kidding? I've been reading you all your life, Murray."

Murray walked over to the row of file cabinets, and tapped one of the drawers with a knuckle. "Help yourself. How about some coffee?"

"Beautiful, Murray. Make it black, Murray."

Murray turned to the Mexican who was between stories at the machine. *"Oye, Jaime, dos cafés. Uno con crema, uno solo."*

"Sí, señor."

I went to work pulling envelopes full of clips from the drawers, and Murray read the rest of the *Voice.* He was very quiet. I could feel his eyes on me as I worked.

There wasn't much in the clips. There usually isn't when you are looking for bankers and other respectable bad guys. There is plenty on movie stars and politicians, because they spend their lives lusting after the spotlight. They want to be in the papers. But the people who really own the world lust after the darkness. So there wasn't much about the Fuentes family. Just enough to get me started.

There was, for example, the story with pictures about the opening of the Avenida Juarez branch of the Banco de Maya in 1964. It showed Don Luis Fuentes standing in the middle of a group, a squat, hard-faced man, with a hairless face that was very dark in the faded newsprint. Beside him, a foot taller, looking dashing and handsome, was a much younger and much thinner Pepe Fuentes. This was the Pepe who had posed with Cardinal Spellman. To Pepe's right was a younger Moya Vargas. Or as the clip called her, Moya Vargas de la Fuentes. All of them, including Moya, were described as Cubans. To the left of Don Luis was another son, Miguel, a blocky clean-shaven man who seemed older than Pepe. He wore a puzzled, tentative expression on his face, and his hair and skin were lighter. He had the kind of formless, unspecific face that always looks vaguely familiar. Behind them were various unidentified people, including two Americans.

"Here's your coffee, Mr. Briscoe."

"Thanks, Murray. Listen, does *Novedades* have a clip file too?"

"Yeah. It's not too good. But they have one."

"Could you ask for some clips for me?"

"Sure."

I wrote some names on a sheet of copy paper.

He stared at the names: "You're doing a piece on Pepe Fuentes?"

"Yeah. Why?"

He called to Jaime and handed him the sheet of copy paper and told him in Spanish to see what he could find in the *Novedades* library downstairs. Then he turned back to me.

"Pepe Fuentes," he said. "You know, it's very weird. Here's a guy who moved his whole operation to New York. Every week he flies back to Mexico for a couple of days. He uses a good airplane. He uses an experienced pilot. And yet the plane explodes. I mean, doesn't that strike you as weird?"

"Yeah. That's one of the reasons I'm here."

"But there's something else weird. I went to school up in San Miguel Allende a couple of years ago. At the institute. You know the typical GI Bill jerkoff number. Right out of the Army and full of Mailer and Hemingway. Well, I met a guy up there, a painter, an American. Nice kind of guy. But a real bad drunk. I mean, slobbering. Legless. The kind of guy who weighs two hundred and thirty pounds and gets shitface every day."

"So what?"

"Well, I also met some girls up there. It's a great place to meet girls. They all come down from Ohio and these other weird places, you know, to paint, and to, you know, get *into* themselves, and all that crap. So when I left last year, and got this job, I kept going back there whenever I could. Just to pick up chicks. Well, I was up there two weeks ago. I was in this joint off the square when this guy Mike came in."

"Sober?"

"Sort of. I mean, for him, he was sober. But he started drinking brandy. Then around one o'clock a kid came around selling the *News*. It's a big market for the *News*. Tourists. Painters. All those old ladies studying ceramics at the Art Institute on the alimony payments."

This kid wasn't bad.

"And?"

"And he picked up the paper and started thumbing through it, grunting, you know, bitching about the whole fucking world." The kid paused. "Then he sees something in the paper, and says 'Oh my God' in English, and stares, and says 'Oh my God' again, this time in Spanish, and then he starts to cry. I mean, I was embarrassed. This great big macho son of a bitch crying his ass off. And he was reading this story. And it was about Pepe Fuentes dying in this crash. It was an AP story, pretty small."

"I read it. Bare as bones."

"Three paragraphs," Murray said. "But it was three paragraphs more than we filed. It costs too much to send out stories these days. At least that's what the bosses say. And this wasn't big enough."

I sipped the coffee. The phone rang, and he picked it up, and started talking in flawless Spanish. A bus had apparently gone off a cliff somewhere near Acapulco. There were forty-five people on board, and when it hit the bottom of the arroyo it burst into flames. That was the nitty-gritty of news. The more dead, the better chance you had of getting into the papers; if the dead included any Americans, you were certain to get in, maybe even get on page one in a lot of places, on the theory that American lives were more valuable than the lives of anyone else on the earth. I made notes from the clips, while Murray worked the phones with the Acapulco cops. I didn't know what kind of a reporter he was, but he was sure asking all the right questions. I hoped he finished quickly, because I wanted to know more about the man named Mike who had cried in the saloon in San Miguel Allende.

Another pile of clips came in from *Novedades*. I thanked Jaime and started riffling through the envelopes. A lot of the clips were junk: pictures of the father opening new branches of the bank in Monterrey, Acapulco, Vera Cruz, Tampico, Ciudad Juarez, even Oaxaca. In the earliest pictures, in the mid-Sixties, the sons were there with the old man. After that, only Don Luis was present. Beside him in each place was the local mayor, or the state governor. And of course, there were pictures of him with Presidents Ordaz and Eccheveria. One long profile in *Excelsior* described his rise to riches since his arrival from Cuba, and said that in Cuba he had been a leading industrialist until the triumph of Fidel. There was even one photograph of him with some of the Cuban fighters who had gone into exile. Ultiminio (Sugar) Ramos, Jose (Mantequilla) Napoles, Angel (Robinson) Garcia. The fighters were all smiling, but Don Luis looked uncomfortable, as he presented one of them with a championship cup from the Cuban-Mexican Friendship Committee.

A magazine story showed the old man at the family home in Las Lomas, the lush residential area that climbed away from the valley floor. The home was beautiful, with an azure pool, a Maillol in the garden, a Tamayo in the living room: a perfect example of the genius of modern Mexican architecture in its use of wood, stone, tezontle, and glass. The old man looked uncomfortable. The old man always looked uncomfortable. In none of the pictures did he have a wife.

I scribbled notes, including the address of the house out in the Lomas.

Murray had stopped taking his notes on the bus

crash, and was writing his story, pounding an old upright Smith-Corona with two fingers, and humming to himself.

I opened the second envelope and spread out the clips on Moya Vargas.

She had lived some kind of life.

In the early pictures, she must have been nineteen, maybe younger. And she is unbelievable: long-legged, with a fine smile, and a face as smooth as butter. She is an actress, the clips say, working on some ranchero picture out at the Churubusco Studios. It is 1960. She poses with various singing cowboys. She poses with a director. She poses with a visiting Italian producer, who says she would be perfect to play one of the Children of Sanchez. She poses with Sam Peckinpah, who is married to another Mexican actress at the time, but says that Moya has a great future. She has a mother, a French-speaking Swiss with a severe face. That would explain the passport. The mother is in some of the pictures. The mother sits with her daughter when the daughter gives an interview on the merits of virginity. It is 1962. She is posing for the same pictures. But her face has begun to settle. The mouth seems a little harder. She talks in one interview about a film she is going to make in Hollywood. But there is no other mention of the picture in Hollywood. We see her sitting at a bar in Acapulco with Marlon Brando and John Huston, and a lot of vaguely familiar people, including a second-rate producer I once knew. It is 1963. She is stopped for reckless driving and taken to a police station in Mexico City at two in the morning, charged with kicking a cop. The story doesn't say she kicked the cop in the balls but her snarling face as she leaves the station with her lawyer makes you think she probably did; she certainly was capable of it. The gossip columns say she is still showing up in all the night spots, and that she has traveled in the spring to Europe, to appear at the Cannes Film Festival. Now there are pictures of her on the beach, in a see-through bikini, with the Mediterranean spread out behind her. She has a lush, almost perfect body, but her face is growing even harder. Even *Siempre*, the left-wing weekly, runs a picture of her in the see-through bikini.

Two months later, in July of 1963, she marries Pepe Fuentes. The wedding is gigantic and formal, with white tie and tails on the men, and the bride in a white gown designed by Christian Dior. The bridesmaids are beautiful, in a silly, giggling way. Moya's mother smiles bleakly, perhaps even triumphantly. Don Luis looks uncomfortable.

In one of the pictures is Pepe's brother, the fair-haired cleanshaven one named Miguel.

The story is familiar and trite, as familiar to Hollywood as it is to Mexico. The clips begin to fall off after that. One small clip announces that she and Pepe have had a child, a baby boy named Roberto. The gossip columns have the couple moving around the world: safaris in Africa, ski trips to Austria. The Banco de Maya opens a branch in Geneva, and Moya's mother poses with Don Luis at the opening ceremonies. She is wearing mink now. Don Luis looks like an old dark Bolshevik, and is, of course, uncomfortable. The young couple also has a house in the Lomas. Pepe starts getting heavier. He masks his face with dark glasses. He waves away a photographer, his face contorted in anger. It is 1970.

Then, tragedy. Pepe and Moya are out for the night at a party and a fire breaks out in their home in Las Lomas. The baby, Roberto, dies. So do two maids, but the maids only make the last paragraph of the story. The son is dead. At the funeral, Pepe and Moya look wasted. Don Luis seems older and more frail. Moya's mother is not there.

For a year, there are no clips.

Then a smaller clip, five paragraphs, announcing the divorce. No explanations.

One final clip tells the faithful readers of the *Novedades* society page that Pepe Fuentes has married Lillian Boney. A *rubia*. The picture shows a shiny blonde woman with a harmless, vacant smile. Pepe is fat now. Moya Vargas, the actress, was the first wife, the story said, but the marriage has since been annulled. Presto. The divorce had become an annulment. It was wonderful to be rich.

"How are you doing?" Murray said.

He startled me.

"Uh, pretty good. Better than I expected."

"Most of those clips are bullshit," he said, looking over my shoulder at the spread of clips. "Press-agent crap."

"What about the facts?"

"The marriage and the rest of it? I guess they're accurate. But that movie and society stuff is usually just garbage in the papers down here."

"You mean society stuff is brilliant and good and reliable up there in the New York papers?"

He laughed. "I guess it's all bullshit."

"Yeah," I said, "except Charlotte Curtis at the *Times*. She's a reporter."

He nodded and jammed his hands in his pockets.

I said: "You had a good one in Acapulco?"

"All Mexicans. I called the bureau chief at home and he said I should file three paragraphs. You know: forty-five dead in Mexico crash. They run it on page fifty-three, under *Doonesbury*."

"Listen, you never finished your story."

"What story?"

"The guy in San Miguel. The guy who cried for Pepe Fuentes."

He looked at his watch. "Hey, I'm through around here. You want to grab a beer somewhere?"

I hefted the file on Pepe Fuentes, which I hadn't had a chance to examine.

"Take them with you," Murray said. "What the hell, nobody's gonna be writing about *him* tonight."

I slipped the envelope into my jacket pocket. Murray waved to Jaime, told him to put the lights out when he left, and we went out.

"To tell the truth, there's not much more," he said in the elevator. "The guy took off, and left his paper there. He was big, like I said, and he bumped into a couple of walls. Crying and sobbing. But when I looked at the paper and saw it was the story about Fuentes, and then came down here the next night and looked at the clips, I knew who the guy was."

"His brother?"

He stared at me.

"Yeah, his brother. Fifty, sixty pounds heavier. Looking like Hemingway with the beard. But his brother."

"Where do you do your drinking, kid?"

14

He did his drinking in a small dark bar on Calle Versailles and he wasn't a very good drinker. His generation just wasn't used to throwing booze down its collective neck, but he did try. Pretty hard. Murray knocked off four fast mezcals, while the Mexican bartender shuffled silently between us and two older Mexicans at the other end of the bar. Behind the cash register a naked Aztec maiden was being sacrificed on an altar. She was on her back and her breasts pointed straight up at the sky, as highly polished as bronze turrets. The calendar was selling Moctezuma beer, so I had one of them in her honor while Murray bombed himself with the mezcal. On the fifth mezcal, he told me again that he had been reading me all his life.

I asked him why he hadn't gone back to San Miguel to find the bearded man.

"No story," he said, in a blurry way. "The guy's dead. This Pepe. There's a feature there maybe, but not for a wire service. Not for me. No story."

"You think so? I mean, even after you came back and looked at those clips?"

"Maybe a magazine piece. Maybe a story for you. A columnist, he can write a story like that. Human stuff. Brother cries at death of brother. That kinda stuff." He drained his glass and slid it toward the barman. "But for a wire service, hey, they don't care, man."

"How do you know? You don't even know what the story is."

His eyebrows moved up, and then fell again. The bartender stared at him out of stony Indian eyes. I drained my beer and nodded for another. I put twenty pesos on the bar. One of the older men got up and put twenty centavos in the jukebox, and started punching buttons.

"What do you think the story is?" Murray said. "If there's a story, what the hell is it? Answer me that."

"I don't know. But I would have gone up there to find out. Were there any clips on the brother?"

"No."

I turned my back on the bartender and the two Mexicans and riffled through the envelope of clips on Pepe Fuentes. There were a lot of duplicates from the file on his father: the same ceremonial bank openings, the wedding to Moya Vargas. But there were also clips on Pepe's second marriage and the birth of two more kids. The father was not in these pictures. And there were clips about the final plane crash, and graphic pictures of Pepe's father and the second wife, Lillian Boney, coming back from the crash site. The father's face is impassive. Lillian is wearing heavy dark glasses and a black raincoat and is leaning on the father's arm. One gossip-column story indicated in a snotty way that father and daughter-in-law had been reconciled by the tragic death of Pepe. There were no quotes to support this statement, but there was a lot of bad writing.

"What do they tell you?" Murray said. He was now balancing himself with four fingertips placed against the edge of the bar. The Mexicans were ignoring us, listening to the jukebox.

"Not a hell of a lot."

He smiled. "You don't understand a wire service, Briscoe. It's not what you do for a living, y'know."

"I worked for one in La Paz for a year. When I was younger than you, Murray."

"Well, then you know. Bastards won't send me cross-town, never mind to San Miguel. Cheap bastards. Keep all the stories to three graphs. Tolstoy got a story about Napoleon? Fine. Keep it to three graphs. You know. Cheap bastards."

"Why didn't you go up there on your own, Murray?"

"Who covers for me in the bureau? You?"

"Don't you have a bureau chief?"

"Yeah. But he spends all his time selling the service to the Mexican papers. The Guatemalan papers. Costa Rica. He's a salesman, not a newspaperman. *I'm* the bureau, Briscoe. *I'm* the fucking bureau."

He was a nice kid but he was starting to bore me; under the surface cynicism there was a whine, and some hostility.

"When did you start drinking mezcal, Murray?"

"I dunno. College? No. Not college. Did grass in college. Hash. Acid a couple a times. Not college. Started mezcal down here. Read about it in some book. Liked the part where it said they kept a worm in the bottom of the bottle."

"Like Original Sin?" I said.

He grinned sloppily. "Something like that."

On the jukebox Cuco Sanchez was singing a song that I knew long ago. It was called "Anillo de Compromiso," and it was all about a wedding ring that some busted-out guy would never get to give to the girl he loved.

"You married, Murray?"

"No. Never got around to it."

I touched his glass with the beer bottle, in a kind of toast. "You know, that stuff you're drinking should only be served with a prescription."

He laughed a little too hard. Cuco Sanchez finished, and the Trio Los Panchos began to sing a song whose tune I knew, but whose words I could no longer remember. The melody made me feel lonely.

"Listen, Murray, where do I find this guy, up there in San Miguel?"

"The brother? The fat-bearded brother?"

"Yeah."

"Just check out the bars. There ain't that many bars. All around the square. Next to the English book store. Try the bars. He's a big bastard, see, with a beard like Hemingway and a Oaxaca sweater. Typecasting, you know. An expatriate. Wipes his ass with *The Sun Also Rises*."

This time I laughed. "Thanks, Murray."

"I read you all my life. Did I tell you that?"

"Yeah? Well, I gotta go home, Murray. You oughtta go home, too."

"Home?" There was a hint of self-pity in him now. "What home? I got no home, man." He turned to the bartender. *"Oye, Chiquito, un mezcal, por favor, y una cerveza mas para mi amigo."*

I wanted to get out of there, but the bartender nodded and pulled an iced beer out of a box and yanked the top off with an opener. Then he filled the mezcal glass, and tapped on the bar with his knuckles, indicating that the round was on the house. I was still enough of a New Yorker to know that you didn't leave a saloon after the house had bought the drinks. Not if you ever wanted to come back.

"Where do you live, Murray? I mean, even if you don't have a home, you must have a place where you go to fall down."

"Street called Ejército Nacional. Over in Palanco."

"I know the street. Big and wide. Tall trees. Lots of traffic." Jesus, I was starting to talk like him. I gulped the beer. His face brightened.

"Yeah, yeah, that's it. You really *do* know it. Shit. You *know* it."

"I lived there once."

His eyebrows did their climbing act again. *"Lived* there? When?"

"A long time ago. There were five of us, all on the GI Bill. Everybody had a room, and we drank too much and argued over who should pay for the toilet paper. It was one of the best times I ever had."

"You lived on Ejército Nacional?" he said numbly, driving a knife into my sentimentality.

"That's what I said, Murray."

He was still trying to digest all of this when a fat hooker walked in, dressed in a tight black satin dress. Her lips glistened. When she saw Murray, she smiled broadly, and a gold tooth glittered in the lights from behind the bar. I knew right then why he hadn't gone to San Miguel.

Murray said, "Ah, ha! Irma la Dulce!"

She came over and put a thick arm around his narrow waist and rubbed her large breasts against his arms. "*Ay, Moo-ray, como estas, mi vida?*"

"*Muy horny, guapa. Qué tu quieres?* What do you want to drink?"

"*El mismo.*"

Murray called to the bartender and told him to bring a double rum for Irma la Dulce with a Coca-Cola on the side. He introduced us and I shook her damp hand and she smiled her gold-toothed smile, and I could see the little girl that was still there under the flesh and I knew Murray wasn't going home to Ejército Nacional. Not that night. Maybe not for a few nights. I sipped my beer, left twenty pesos on the bar as a tip, murmured that I had to do some work, said good night to Murray, winked at Irma la Dulce and went out into the night.

Walking up the Reforma to the hotel, I felt drained and tired. I thought about all the details I had read in the clips, and what Murray had told me of the large man who cried for the death of his brother in a saloon in San Miguel. That large man had lived for a while in newspaper clippings and then was suddenly gone. I thought of Anne Fletcher being lowered into the snowy ground half a continent away, and the spook, the pulpy man who had trailed me around New York and whom I had left shivering in the snow. I tried to remember everything that Moya Vargas had told me that night in her place in Brooklyn Heights and what she had left out. And something started to take shape in my head: an idea, a pattern, a form for all the details. But some of it was too personal, still too fragmented into shards of my own past. I could not yet stand outside it, and see it as a story. And I was too drowsy with beer and altitude and the slow, dull shock of the return to Mexico to put it all together. I would go to the hotel and sleep for a long time, and then I would be ready to think.

At the Geneva, the management had finally changed desk clerks. The gruff older man was gone, and in his place was a young man in his twenties, with shirt sleeves that were too long or jacket sleeves that were too short, a soiled tie, and a nervous mouth. He told me there were no phone messages. He handed me the key and told me to use the side elevator, because the main elevator was being repaired. I walked down a corridor, past the bulging wall racks outside the door of the travel bureau, all the folders offering trips to the pyramids, and weekends in Cozumel, and afternoons at the bullfights. The light bulbs in the corridor were dim. There was a fire door, leading to a stairwell, and an old service elevator down in the corner. I pressed the button for the elevator and went up two floors.

I let myself in with the key. The bed light was on, and the bedding was turned down. The room and the bed looked inviting. The room had a faint odor of gardenias. I hung my jacket in the standing closet and draped my shirt and trousers over one of the chairs beside the card table. If I were to do this right, I thought, I should sit at the typewriter and turn everything into notes, four or five pages of single-spaced, densely written facts. The writing of the notes would reveal the story. But I was too tired for any of that. It could wait. Almost anything could wait.

I opened the door to the bathroom.

The walls were spattered with blood. My shaving kit was on the floor. Beside it was a woman's stocking and a bra that was stained with blood. The door to the medicine cabinet was off its hinges. A pair of panties were in the toilet bowl.

I pulled the shower curtain aside.

She was lying in the tub, with her legs up. Her blouse had been ripped open, and her bare young breasts were wet with blood. Her skirt was shoved up in a bunched ridge above her smooth thighs. There was no water in the tub, but the bottom was sticky with blood, faeces and urine.

It was hard to see her face, because her head had flopped back over the edge of the tub. Her mouth and eyes were wide open in shock.

It was the Carter kid.

Someone had cut her throat, right through to the bone.

15

I didn't know who had done it to her, or even, really, who she was. But right away I knew it was a set-up. And I was the party being set up.

So I didn't call the front desk. I certainly didn't call the cops. I knew the laws of Mexico too well. They operated under the Napoleonic Code. You were guilty until proven innocent. And once, a long time before, I had been arrested in Mexico City after a terrible brawl in a whorehouse, and had gone to jail. I was still out on bail six months later when I skipped the country owing them time. It was one of the reasons I had not been back. I was certain the jails had not gotten better since I had last been inside.

And this was my room. I had the key. My fingerprints were probably all over the place. The desk clerk who worked the day shift would probably testify, three months from now, or six months from now, whenever they took me out of my dungeon, that I had made a point of asking whether a Miss Carter had checked in. The wet-lipped stewardess from Aeronaves would say that I had spent a long time on a long flight from New York talking to the girl. It was hard to forget a girl with tangerine hair. Someone might even find those old police records of what I had done when I was a kid, and discover that I was a fugitive from Mexican justice. I could spend a couple of years in the Black Palace of the Lecumberri trying to prove that I hadn't killed anyone. Or, if someone powerful enough was mad enough, I could find myself shot dead while trying to escape.

So I started to get dressed. The set-up was too perfect. The door had not been forced, so the killer had to have a key. Both desk clerks would say that I had used the key. But obviously someone else had picked up a key. If he was a fellow gringo, that might not have been too difficult, if he had walked in boldly and just asked for it. And there was always *la mordida*, the true governor of Mexico, the bite, the bribe. He could have gotten the key for a hundred pesos, with no questions asked. And if the clerk had indeed taken a bribe and the bribe had led to a murder, he would not be prepared to admit it, and thus face arrest as an accessory. His memory of the truth would begin to fail. In a trial, I could always bring in Murray, of course, who would tell the judge that I was with him all the time; but that would have about the same effect that one friendly Puerto Rican witness has in a trial of another Puerto Rican charged with homicide in New York. It would be my word and Murray's against the word of a respectable Mexican desk clerk in a respectable Mexican hotel. Next case.

I finished dressing and then packed, putting the briefcase inside the larger bag. I lifted my shaving kit off the sticky floor, wiped it clean with a towel, laid it beside the briefcase, and zippered the bag shut. Then I wiped off as many surfaces as possible, including the handle of the bathroom door.

I took one last look at poor Nicola Carter.

The taut dancer's legs were locked in the jagged final position of death. A sad little triangle of dark red hair was showing between her legs and I pulled down her skirt to cover her. The gesture of a Jew who had gone to Catholic schools. Her helmet of tangerine hair was twisted and mussed, revealing ears as small and neat as a baby's. Whoever had done this had held her by that hair while he ripped her. I remembered the story she had told me so easily on the plane, about the mad comedian she had married, and his violence and jealousy, a story that was too simple and too easy to be completely believable. There was probably a man in her life, and he was probably not much different from the man she had

described. But he could not have come down here to
Mexico so swiftly, to slaughter her in my room. He
could have done that in New York, in a hundred
different places and a thousand different ways, and
been a lot safer than he would be in a strange country. No, this was someone who was more concerned
with me than he was with Nicola Carter. Someone
who had sent her to that airplane at the last moment,
to find me, to tell me a sad story, to spend time with
me and keep track of what I was doing. I took a
washcloth off the rack and covered my hand with it
while I flicked out the light and closed the bathroom
door.

Then I moved my bag and typewriter to the door,
and switched off the lights. I waited. Listening. I
heard nothing. I opened the door an inch and peered
out. The hall looked empty, except for some scattered
pairs of shoes waiting to be shined.

I wiped the inside doorknob with the washcloth,
and stepped out into the hall, carrying the typewriter
and suitcase. I put them down and closed the door.
I locked it with the large key and then wiped the
outside knob, and put the washcloth in my pocket.
My heart was pounding.

I walked to the fire door, and went down to the
lobby level. I opened the door a crack. Someone in
a back office was playing a radio very softly. The
tourist agency was directly across from the fire door.
I darted across the hall and emptied the racks of
their folders, stuffing a lot of them in my pockets, and
holding the others tightly to my chest. I went back to
the fire stairs and up two flights. I stepped carefully
into the hall, and started moving from door to door,
gently trying the handles.

Near the end of the hall, I found one that was
open.

I went in and switched on the lights.

Empty.

The pounding in my heart did not stop.

I dumped all the folders into a waste basket,

bunching and balling them loosely. I added a lot of onionskin hotel stationery from the desk. Then I moved the waste basket over to the windows and put the end of one of the curtains into the basket.

I lit the paper with my lighter.

Then I slammed the door behind me, and ran to the main stairwell, and started shouting.

"Fuego! Fuego! Ayúdame! Fuego!" Then, in English. "Fire! Help! Help!"

I ran down the hall to the fire stairs, hurried down the two flights and waited. If the hotel people decided to use the fire stairs I was fucked. The gamble was that they would use the elevator to go to the second floor. I heard footsteps running, people shouting about fire, an alarm starting to ring. And they ran past me. To the elevator.

I cracked open the door and listened. The elevator jerked into motion. I stepped out and walked briskly to the main desk. The door on the side was open, where the night clerk had run out, and the radio was still playing. I heard muffled shouts from the direction of the main stairwell. I put the bags down and went into the office. It was empty.

I wiped the key with the washcloth and put it back in its slot behind the front desk. Then I looked at the roster of hotel guests and removed my registration card. In the message box there was an envelope with my name on it. I felt it. The passport. I put it in my jacket pocket, and then went back to the office. The alarm was really clanging now. On a desk there was a long metal file tray, with the word "Huespedes" handlettered on its front. Guests. I opened it and looked for my name and found the carbon of my registration form, and then stepped around to the cashier's file and yanked my card from that file too.

I stepped out of the office, and closed the door behind me. Then the front door opened. A group of cops and firemen came rushing up the stairs into the lobby. Some of them had fire extinguishers, but I could see a fire truck outside and firemen unreeling hose. I tried to look like a baffled tourist.

"Up there!" I said, pointing to the main stairwell. "A big fire. El fire. El smoke-o."

They ran to the main stairs. I picked up my bags and went outside. The fire truck was double-parked and the firemen were working frantically to unspool hose and get the water working. A police car blocked traffic, its blue signal light whirling frantically, illuminating the small crowd of pimps and tourists who were drifting up from the corners. The cops ignored me. I saw a cab near the corner and jumped in.

"Chingada Hotel," I muttered in Spanish. "I was just checking in and the place goes on fire."

"Oh, *coño* . . ."

"So take me to a hotel, driver."

"Big American hotel?"

"No. Small Mexican hotel. Somewhere central."

"You know the Maria Cristina?" he said.

"Perfect."

The Maria Cristina was one of those small gems that you forget about when you move around too much. Twenty years before I had stayed there with an Ohio State girl one glorious weekend, on the proceeds of a crap game with a few marks from some other Midwest school, and I was shocked that it still existed. So many other good things had vanished off the earth.

"I didn't know it was still there," I said.

"They tell me better than ever."

"*Bueno,*" I said. "*Vámonos.*"

He drove slowly out of the Zona Rosa. I heard sirens. He turned on Avenida Insurgentes and crossed the Reforma and moved up toward the monument to the Independence. The angel at the top of the long shaft was painted gold and bathed in light. It was one of those empty rhetorical boasts of a monument, promising redeeming angels out of the blood of revolution; now everybody in Mexico knew that there were no angels, and there had been no revolution. Just rich people who opened banks and left death lying around them.

I had to ring the bell on the iron gate three times before anyone answered. It was worth the wait. The lobby was clean and cool, with a Christmas tree at the far end providing the only light, except for the muted cowl lamp behind the main desk. The clerk signed me in and didn't ask for my passport. Then he carried my bags up a flight of marble steps to a second floor room. The room was painted white with exposed wooden beams and massive Spanish furniture. I looked out the window into a patio filled with flamboyan trees. There was another Christmas tree in the center of the patio, its lights blinking cheerfully.

The clerk started to leave and I called him back and gave him a hundred-peso bill and told him to bring me a bottle of whiskey. Any kind? Any kind, I said. It doesn't matter. He bowed gravely and went out, knowing everything he had to know about me. I sat on the edge of the bed, thinking that it was two days before Christmas, and I was a long way from home, and the only thing white I had seen was the bone that showed through the blood of a young woman's neck and I knew I was going to have a hell of a time trying to get to sleep.

16

I woke to the sound of metal against metal, as a key turned loosely in a lock.

The drapes were tightly drawn and the room was still dark. I had no idea of the time. I stiffened, held my breath, and groped for something that wasn't there: a gun or a sap or a bottle.

The light snapped on.

A blocky Indian woman in a starched green maid's uniform stood there blinking at me impassively. I exhaled hard and lay back on the lumpy pillow. She smiled and excused herself and I told her it was no problem. No problem. I was getting up now anyway. No problem. *Perdóneme, señor.* It's all right, no problem.

I asked her what time it was. She said it was a few minutes short of eleven. *Bueno.* I told her I would be out of the room in twenty minutes. She excused herself for the ninth time and I told her again it was no problem. And she went out.

I lay there for a full minute, thinking that it was time to start looking for a gun.

I got up slowly. My hair was matted. My tongue was thick. The bottle stood on the top of the bureau across the room, where I'd left it. The liquid looked rancid in the wan afternoon light. It wasn't much of a whiskey but it had been good enough to get me to sleep.

I took the toothpaste and brush into the shower with me and brushed for a long time while the water pounded my body. I looked down once at the tiled floor of the shower, and was happy that the water was

clear, and not pink and orange with blood. While I
was dressing, I called Murray.

"How are you?" I asked him.

"I feel good," he said, sounding terrible.

"You looked like you were in love when I
left."

"Shut up and talk," he said.

"I need a favor."

"I don't know if I can finish a *sentence*, never mind
do a favor."

"I need a car."

"They got Hertz and Avis and Budget Rent-A-
Hearse, and Christ knows how many others. It's
easy."

"I want it in your name," I said. "And I can't tell
you why."

"Well shit, I'll loan you my car. It's got cancer,
but it still goes."

"Can I have it around three?"

"Sure."

I asked him to meet me at the Glorieta Bookstore in Las Lomas, and then I went out to eat.

The seafood place on Rio Lerma wasn't there anymore so I walked down Calle Sullivan, looking for a
place that twenty years ago was called the Super
Cocina. The British Book Store was gone too, but the
Super Cocina was still there. This was like finding an
old girl who was still intact. It was a high-ceilinged
open place, with large brass pots full of food. You
ordered by pointing. I pointed at rice and shrimp,
and a bottle of Carta Blanca, paid, and sat outside at
a tin-topped table. A newsboy came along and I
bought a paper. Nicola Carter was on page one, com-
plete with all the gory details. The story said that
police were looking for a Yankee tourist, whose
description sounded vaguely like me. They didn't
have my name. I knew they didn't have it, because if
they had had it they would have used it. The Mexican
crime reporters use everything, including things that

never happened. I finished the food quickly and walked back to the Maria Cristina. I had a good stiff belt of the whiskey and lay down and slept. The food, the beer and the picture of Nicola made me want to blank out the world.

It was 2:45 when I woke up.

I hurried downstairs and grabbed a cab and gave the driver the address of the bookstore in Las Lomas. Twenty years ago this December the day might have been beautiful, but now it had a feeling of impending catastrophe, as if the whole city was burning somewhere in the outer districts, or under the sidewalks, or in secret tunnels, and the flame was moving inexorably toward those of us who were trapped in the center. The air was pebbly with smog. The driver smoked Alas cigarettes, made of black tobacco, and coughed a lot. My eyes watered. In Mexico. Where the air was clear.

Something was burning.

Pepe had burned. They had found him in the wreckage and then took him back to Mexico City and burned . . . him. And right there, in the cab going to Las Lomas, I knew that something was wrong. Jarringly wrong. As wrong as any lie is wrong. Pepe was a Catholic. His picture had been taken with Cardinal Spellman. There were priests in all the photographs taken with his family. Before he married his second wife, he had even gone to the trouble of having the first marriage annulled.

He was a Catholic.

A Catholic would not have been cremated.

Son of a bitch.

Murray was standing in front of the bookstore, yawning in the smoggy haze, when I pulled up in the cab. I paid the driver and got out.

"You're late," he said.

"I was wrestling at the Arena Mexico. Won two falls out of three against El Angel Enmascarado."

"Yeah? He's a friend of mine."

"He wrestles good, for a Jewish intellectual," I said.

Murray smiled.

"Feel like a drink?"

"No, I'm driving."

"There's only a quarter of a tank of gas in there. That's Pemex for you. Our great national monopoly. You ask them to fill the tank, and they do, but not with gas. Half of it is water."

"Nationalization does it all the time. There's just no way socialism is going to work, is there?"

He laughed and handed me the keys.

"Not in one country. Drive me to the office."

I dropped Murray at the office on Bucareli and then went back to Calle Lerma, a block from the Maria Cristina. I parked the car on a sidestreet, paid an old man two pesos to watch it for me, and went into the hotel. No, there were no messages. Yes, I could check out immediately. I packed the bag, tipped the maid, and carried bag, typewriter and briefcase to the street. Then I hailed a cab and told the driver to take me to Melchor Ocampo and Rio Tiber, about ten blocks away. He left me on the corner. I went into the Tienda Tiber and bought a small bottle of cherry soda and a bag of potato chips, and ate them standing under the awning. The sky was darkening; it felt like rain. That would be good. If it rained, the city would stop burning.

When I finished the soda I went out on Melchor Ocampo and grabbed another cab. He took me to Rio Lerma. I paid him, and looked at newspapers at the corner stand until he was gone. Then I went to the car, opened the trunk, put the suitcase and the typewriter into the back, and took the briefcase, with the tape recorder inside, to the front. If the cops were looking for me I wasn't going to make it easy for them.

I drove out to the university to kill some time

until it got dark, and parked the car outside a small shopping center. In the American-style supermarket, I bought a pair of sunglasses, and a cheap baseball hat. The late editions were up. The headlines were huge. Pictures showed Nicola Carter lying in the bathtub of the Geneva Hotel. Her body looked destroyed. The stories said the police were looking for a gringo but they still didn't have a name.

I wandered around the university in my baseball hat and my shades, looking at the murals by Siquieros and Juan O'Gorman, trying to remember the name of a girl student I knew here years ago. Her father was Mexican and rich and her mother was French and middle-class and she had clear luminous skin and hair like a strawberry roan. I loved her for a week and a half, and then one night she told me not to come around anymore, because her father did not approve. That night I went to her home in San Angel and threw a chunk of poisoned meat over the wall for the guard dogs. I was a much meaner bastard then. Now I was just a character who left naked agents in snowdrifts.

I walked around for almost an hour, thinking that any one of these lovely young girls, holding hands with their young men, could have been her daughter. Or mine. I angled around, tiring finally of murals and architecture, and went back toward the car.

A cop was staring at the car.

I backed up, and stepped into a small coffee shop filled with students. I sat near a window and ordered coffee and a *bolillo*, and listened to the sound of huapango music from Vera Cruz coming off the jukebox, and looked casually at the cop. He reached around the car finally, and grabbed a kitten. He stood there in his brown uniform, stroking the tiny lost animal, while kids on Hondas whizzed by. I ordered another coffee, and after a while, when the cop had left with his kitten, went to the car and drove out of the university.

Her name was Yolanda.

I couldn't remember her last name, and it didn't matter anymore. But I remembered the guard dogs and the poisoned meat.

17

That night I sat for two hours in the dark in the parked car, staring down the hill of Calle Tepeyac in Las Lomas. On the right, behind a high blue-tiled wall, I could see the Japanese lanterns of a garden party, and heard mariachi music, and knew from the huge number of parked cars that something or someone was being celebrated. It was still too early for Christmas here, which in my time was celebrated on the Day of the Three Kings. So it was a birthday, an anniversary, or some other moment of time that called for music. From where I sat, higher up the hill under the dense branches of a plane tree, the music sounded heavy, thick, palpable, the voice of the lead singer breaking out over the walls, the horns attacking in painful tinny choruses. It was the music of the Mexican night, but it meant nothing to me anymore.

I was looking at the house across the street.

The house lay behind a sixteen-foot wall whose sides were smoothed over with a concrete skim. The top of the wall was laced with shards of broken glass. I could see the tops of trees behind the wall, but not a single branch reached out to the street, to invite illicit entry. There were two solid iron gates at the main entrance, and when I had walked past them on an early evening reconnaissance, I had heard the snarling whine of Doberman pinschers. Now, lights glowed dimly from behind the wall. The street that cut in at a right angle above the house was like the street below the house: a dead end, leading to a walled-off arroyo that dropped away into brambles

and rocks. So the house was fortified. And that was
only natural. It belonged to Don Luis Fuentes.

Earlier in the evening I had tried to get a phone
number for the house from information, but the operator told me it was unlisted. And when I had tried
the bell, on my small reconnaissance, nobody had
answered, although I could hear the scrape of huaraches against gravel in the driveway and dogs barking viciously beyond the iron gate. I knew then that
I would have to do what cops and reporters spend
most of their time doing: I waited. I waited a long
time.

I waited until the ambulance made its way slowly up the street, as if the driver were searching tenta-
tively for the address. It was a long blue-and-white
ambulance, with a driver whose skin was the color of a
Brazil nut. He stopped at the iron door, and tapped
the horn: bop-bop-ba-dop-dop-dop. As if it were a
signal. I slid deeper into the seat behind the wheel,
peering over the top of the dashboard, the window
open beside me so that I could still hear. The iron
door opened, its hinges squeaking slightly in the chill
night air. The ambulance moved through the gates
and into the grounds. The doors were swiftly shut.
Trumpets played sadly in the other garden.

The ambulance did not stay long. Within fifteen
minutes, the gate opened, and the ambulance came
out. There were curtains drawn over the back windows and a lighter-skinned *mestizo* was now driving.
I could hear a mariachi trumpet reaching for some
impossible note, faltering, falling back, then calling
for the finish. The ambulance moved down Calle
Tepeyac.

I put my car in gear and eased out from under
the plane tree, with the lights off. I stayed a full
block behind them. They moved down Tepeyac and
out onto the Reforma to the Petroleos Monument, and
then moved off to the right, staying on main streets
all the way. As they joined the stream of traffic at the
Petroleos, I turned on my lights.

The streets grew emptier as they went deeper into the city. A young girl with scraggly hair and a baby lashed to her back moved along the sidewalk of one street, her eyes focused on the distance. The ambulance crossed her path. I waited for her to cross, wondered what would happen to her, and where she had come from and where she was going with her small human baggage, and then went after the ambulance again. It was going at medium speed. On Avenue Chapultepec, it turned right. I waited for a stoplight. A few fat hookers with charcoal-dark eyes stared from the window of a small bar. When the light changed and I turned, the ambulance was gone.

I moved along slowly, staring at the buildings. The street was lined with four-story stone houses, once the proud homes of the Mexican aristocracy, now largely chopped up into cheap flats. One of them looked in better condition than the others. Lights glowed behind curtains on the upper floors. A ledge ran around the building under the windows. A yellow bulb burned over the gates to its driveway, which must have led to an old carriage house for horses. I pulled around the block, parked behind a line of other cars, locked the doors, and got out. My legs were bunched from the hours of sitting, and I did some squats to loosen them.

I went to the gate with the yellow light and rang a buzzer. Seconds went by. A few blocks away, I saw a police car cruising along slowly, its parking lights like dim orange eyes. I wondered if the orange eyes were searching for a gringo who had run a knife through a girl's neck in the bathtub of a second-class hotel. I buzzed again.

A bolt moved on the far side of the gate, and then the gate swung open. A short fat man with glittering gold teeth smiled at me.

"*Buenas noches, señor,*" he said, and bowed me into the yard.

"*Buenas noches,*" I said, and walked in like a shy, slightly ashamed tourist.

The ambulance was parked with other cars along
the far wall of the yard. The back door was open. The
man with the nut-brown face sat on the bumper,
smoking. And from behind a door, I could hear music.
The short fat man closed the gate and locked it behind me. I heard a woman's laugh from an upper
floor.

The whorehouse was packed. In the large central room on the first floor were all the faces of the
city: fat girls, thin girls, short girls, tall girls, girls in
evening gowns and girls in chemises, girls with pow-
dered flour-white faces and Indian girls stained with
rouge, old girls and little girls, and moving through
them were boys with sallow night-side faces, and old
men with snowy hair, and heavy-set gunsels in sharkskin suits; broken-nosed guys who smelled of co-
logne, and sidestreet dudes with Vaselined hair and
pouchy eyes and white ridges in the dark skin where
razors had passed on evenings long ago. They were
four deep at the bar against the far wall, and the
women moved among them, embracing them, coiling
around them, murmuring to them, laughing with
them and sometimes at them, while the romantic
music of a guitar trio oozed like syrup in the other
corner. Once in a while a man would split away from
the group, taking the hand of a girl, and they would
move through curtains to a stairway that climbed to
the upper floors. I went to the bar and reached in
and ordered a beer. A few dark faces looked at me,
but without any particular hostility. They were all
drinking and happy, surrounded by women who were
at their command, as long as there was money and
enough time to spend it. It was nice to be in a country
where the whorehouses were glad and noisy, instead
of furtive and sad.

A girl touched my arm. *"Como estás, señor?"*

"How are you?" I said, in Spanish.

She was about twenty, with a long aquiline nose

in a thin face, too much rouge and a blouse cut low over small breasts.

"Do you want to go upstairs?" she whispered in Spanish.

"In a while," I said. "Can I buy you a drink?"

"*Sí, sí. Un whiskey?*"

"*Como te llamas?*" I said, motioning for the attention of the bartender.

"Rosa."

Of course. Rosa. They were always called Rosa. Rosa with the rosy red ass. Rosa with a rose in her teeth, clicking her castanets. Rosa. Or Carmen. Carmen was another big name. Same act. I ordered a whiskey for her and it came back very thin, like the drinks they used to sell in the bars of Tu Do Street in Saigon. Saigon tea. Part of the great buying and selling and whoring called war. Another group of men came in, four or five of them, in their thirties, full of macho swagger, grabbing at the girls, and Rosa's eyes looked at them the way you might look at meat in a marketplace. I sipped my beer and gently squeezed her hand.

"*Ahora,*" I said. Now. Now was as good a time as any. Now. *Ahora.* How much was it? One hundred pesos, *señor. Bueno.* A hundred pesos. Why not? *Ahora.* Now.

She led me through the curtains and up the stairs with the music fading behind us. I was looking for someone in this place and I wasn't even sure who it was. I knew it was nobody who was physically sick, nobody who needed an ambulance.

The second floor was lined with doors, leading to the cribs, and there was a smell of incense in the air. I tried a door, and it did not open, and Rosa grabbed my hand. No, *señor.* No. Do not bother the customers. Follow me. Of course, Rosa. I'll follow you. I heard a deep low groan of orgasm from behind a door, the sound of middle-aged relief and helplessness. The music from the downstairs bar sounded as if it were in the next building.

Then, at the far end of the long hall, a door opened. A large-breasted girl with tousled hair and pouting lips and skin the color of cinnamon walked out, vaguely smiling.

Behind her was a heavy-set man with a moustache and powerful arms, wearing a sportshirt and trousers.

It was Pepe Fuentes.

He blinked. I didn't.
"Hello, Pepe," I said.
He blinked again.
I smiled.

He grunted and swung, and I pulled away, but not quickly enough. The punch hit me high on the cheekbone, and something hot moved back in my head, and when I turned, he hit me again. I reached for him, and heard a shout, and a girl screaming, and I grabbed something in the blur and started to punch. I hit something soft, and then was hit again. Someone had me by the arm and was pulling me, and I could hear men running up the stairs, and then I was in a room. Rosa was beside me, opening a window and shoving me out on the ledge.

"*Váyate, váyate*, go, go," she said.

And I was on the eight-inch ledge outside the row of rooms on the second floor and I looked down, my head clearing in the chill of the night air. The gate was open, the ambulance moving to it.

I jumped.

And landed on the roof of the ambulance.

The driver suddenly gunned the engine, driving flat-out and hard through the gates. He veered to the right, trying to swing me off the roof, but I grabbed a runner along the side and held on. At the corner he jerked hard to the right, trying again. But I held on. There was no sign of the cops and their orange eyes. The ambulance turned right, and left.

Then the first shot tore through the roof. The

metal burst up and out. And then another. I scrambled for a different position, holding to the runner.

They were heading for a dark, badly lit street. A car was double-parked at the corner and as the ambulance slowed to pass, another shot tore through the roof, and this time I rolled, and dropped off. Go. Go on, Pepe. I'll see you later.

I hit the pavement hard, ran the first few steps, feeling as if the gutter was jamming itself through my knees, started to go down, reached out and touched a parked car and steadied myself and then stopped.

I was alone on the street.

With all the turns and the shooting I wasn't certain where I was and where I had left my car. I walked quickly to the corner. I saw a police car coming fast in the distance, blue light whirling on its roof, and I faded back into the darkened street. I didn't want to sit in any cell that night, explaining that I hadn't slaughtered Nicola Carter in that bathtub. I didn't want to explain anything. I ducked into a doorway. The police car slowed, and I felt as if the cops were looking down the street right at me. But they weren't. They kept moving.

I started walking back to the next block. If the main street, where the cops were, was Chapultepec, then my car was parked somewhere to the left, a block or two behind me. I would find the car, go back to Las Lomas and wait. But for now I was safe. Then, as I reached the corner, two giant lights crashed on. It was the ambulance. I was framed in the blinding, sudden light. And then it came right up on the sidewalk, racing at me, and I grabbed the handle of a door beside me. Locked. Moved back another three or four feet. Walls. Nothing. No door, no escape, the car gunning at me, twenty feet away. Ten feet away. About to die.

And then I dove.

Forward.

Under the car.

My hands over my head.

Something scraped the knuckles of my right hand, gears screamed into my ears, the exhaust gassed me, and then the car was gone. It had passed right over me.

I lay there as if I were dead.

And heard another two shots. Blam. Blam. Just like that. Deliberate. Spaced. And a bullet bounced off the sidewalk beside me. And then another one. I shuddered, twitched, and lay still, as if they had hit me.

I heard the car roaring away.

I lay there.

And slowly opened my eyes, and looked down an empty street.

I got up, and started moving quickly, hugging the wall, jogging, then running. I didn't stop running until I'd found the car. I got in behind the wheel and locked the door behind me, and dropped out flat on the floor.

I lay there for a long time.

18

In Mexico City, they say you can buy anything on the street called San Juan de Letran: women, boys, diseases, politicians, goats, a lot of other things. If you have the money, they have the goods. I parked the car on the Street of the Lost Child and walked over to San Juan de Letran and did some shopping. A meat market, a *farmacia*, the corner table of a certain bar, and in an hour I was finished. I went back to the car and drove to Chapultepec, and parked across the street, and a block away, from the house with the yellow lights. I waited for almost two hours, but the girl named Rosa never came out. I wished she would. I wanted to thank her for doing something she had really no reason to do. I wanted to kiss her. Or, if that would make her happy, give her money.

But after two hours, I couldn't wait any longer. I drove up to Las Lomas, moving past Tepeyac up the Reforma, and coming around behind the hill. I opened one of the packages, and pushed six cartridges into the .38-caliber Smith and Wesson semiautomatic. I tucked the other packages under my arm, locked the car and went out.

I found a street called Ajijic, a block above the Fuentes house, turned left and walked to the low concrete block barrier at the end of the street that overlooked the arroyo. I scaled the wall.

The arroyo sloped away at a steep angle, but there was a path at the foot of the wall. A ways off, dogs were barking. I moved along the path and when I reached the back of the Fuentes house, the wall got much higher, rising to about twenty feet. And the dogs barked more loudly, and with a hungry, vicious snarl to the barking. I wondered if they were Dobermans. I wondered if I had once knocked off their grandfathers, in anger over a girl named Yolanda.

I opened the second package, shook the can of arsenic over the six slabs of meat, and then tossed them, one at a time, over the wall. The dogs barked and gnashed and then were quiet. I could hear ripping sounds, tooth against bone. I drifted down the side of the arroyo, propped myself against a wall, and waited. The .38 was jammed in my belt.

While I waited, I unwrapped the third package, and took out the hook and the nylon rope. The hook had three prongs, turned in like claws. I slipped the rope through the hoop, knotted it, hefted it, and moved back up the slope and tossed it over the wall. I pulled gently, letting it drag until it found something. A crevice, a piece of decorative wood. Something. And it hooked something. And held. I pulled on it, bracing myself, knowing that it had to hold 200 pounds of Irish Jew. When it felt right, I took off my jacket, tucked it into the back of my belt, slipped the .38 in my pocket, put my feet against the wall, pulled hard and started up.

For a moment, the rope started to slip. I waited, expecting to fall, imagining the glass knifing through the nylon. But the hook dug into something, and held. I scrambled to the top. Doubling the rope around my left hand, I whipped the jacket out of my belt, and forced it over the shards of broken beer bottles that had been planted in the concrete top. I boosted myself onto the coat. Some longer shards stabbed through the coat, and I stamped them flat with the heel of my shoe. Then I looked around.

The house lay behind a row of flamboyan trees, blazing now in their brief sad season. The house lights were still on. Below me lay four dead dogs. They were all Dobermans. There was no sign of the ambulance. I pushed down on the hook, which had dug into a strip of wooden planking, removed it, and jammed it hard into a nick on the outside of the wall, letting the rope dangle into the inside of the grounds. Then I went down the rope, dropping the last four feet to the ground. I landed among the dead dogs.

The impact jarred my legs, already sore from the fall from the ambulance, and I got up slowly.

A man was walking toward me.

He was carrying a rifle, his head down, humming a melody.

I stepped behind a tree.

He reached the tree, and I skulled him with the pistol. He fell with a gurgling sound. I kicked him in the head to keep him out. I took his rifle with me, and moved through the dark pools of shadow to the house. I shoved the rifle under a bush and peeped into the brightly lit main living room.

Don Luis Fuentes was sitting before a fireplace, reading a book. He was wearing a silk robe. There were many paintings on the walls, including one that looked like a Delacroix, and there were lush plants everywhere. The window was filmy with steam, as if the old man were living in a hothouse.

I looked into the room adjoining the living room. A heavyset brown man sat with his feet up on a plain table, reading a comic book. There was a rifle on the table. He was smoking a cigar. There were no other lights on in the building. I moved to the plate glass windows along the bedroom wall, and around to a side door leading to a laundry room. The door was open. It must have been the door from which the other guard had gone out for his painful walk. I slipped into the laundry room, past tubs and an electric drier, and opened the second door. I was in the house.

I found myself in a long hall. At the far end, I could see part of the living room. The guard was inside the first room on my side of the living room. His door was slightly ajar. There were other doors, apparently leading to bedrooms, all of them closed. Very quietly, I went to the guard's room.

There was no point in wasting time. Holding the gun in my right hand, I jerked the door open with the left, rushed in, and smashed the guard in the face before he had a chance to say anything. He fell over heavily, the cigar under him, the chair making a crashing sound as it hit the tiled floor. I took the rifle, stepped over the guard, and went into the living room.

Don Luis was rising slowly from his chair, the book closing in his lap. He looked pale and doomed, as if he had been expecting someone for a long time, and the someone had finally arrived.

"Who are you?" he said in Spanish, trying unsuccessfully to present a facade of outrage.

"Sit down."

"What are you doing in my house?"

"Sit down," I said, "or I'll knock you down."

He sat down.

"Now don't move or I'll kill you. I have one thing to do."

"I understand," he said.

I went back to the guard's room, rummaged in the drawers, found a maid's closet and located some clothesline. I tied the guard's hands and feet and stuffed a washcloth in his mouth. Still holding the rifle, I kicked open the doors of all the bedrooms. They were all empty. Don Luis was in the great, lush, gaudy house alone, with his useless guard.

I went back to the living room. He hadn't moved.

"Can I get you a drink?" he said. The room was very hot.

"No. You can only tell me the truth. If you don't, I'll kill you."

"What does it matter?" he said with a shrug. "I am an old man."

"In that case, it's not whether I kill you, but how. Dying can be painful, Don Luis."

"Who are you?"

"That doesn't matter."

"Well, then, what do you want?"

"I want to know everything. I want to know where your son is. I want to know what happened to your bank in New York, and where the money is. I want to know why at least two people are dead, including a girl I used to know. I want to know where Moya Vargas is. I want it all, Don Luis."

He stared at me and said nothing.

I went over and slapped him hard. His papery skin quivered from the blow.

"Start talking, *viejo*." I looked at the fireplace. "Or I'll put you in *that*."

His eyes looked runny now. He glanced at the fire, then at the book that lay at his feet. It was *The Edge of the Storm* by Agustin Yanez. He looked like a man who knew that he might never read a book again in peace.

"I don't know what you're talking about," he said quietly.

I grabbed him roughly by the neck with one hand, and lifted him, pushing his face toward the fireplace. Hair crackled in the heat.

"Stop!"

I released the grip.

The old man felt small and frail as I led him to the big chair, and shoved him down.

"All right," I said. "All of it. And fast. I don't have much time."

He sat down, and composed himself, and then he started to talk, the words hesitant at first, his elegant Spanish mixing with his cruder English, occasionally groping for words, speaking low and then rising to a pitch. I sat on the ledge beside the fireplace with the rifle trained at his heart.

"I don't know who you are," he said. "I only know you have that gun. So I speak to the gun. Not to you. You ask about my son. I ask you which one? Do you mean my son Rafael? Well, that son, who was the youngest, was the first to die. In 1961. At the Bay of Pigs. Rafael, who was only twenty. Rafael with the soft brown eyes. Rafael, who read 'The Count of Monte Cristo' in English, when he was ten years old, coming to me every evening in the old country, to tell me where Edmund Dantes was at that moment in his own history. That was Rafael. He cried when we left Havana in 1960. He vowed to return. And return he did, the following year. And there was no air cover. And they were waiting for him and the others because the filthy American reporters had warned them. And Rafael was killed, shot down in the swamp. Is that the son, is that the one you mean, rifle?"

"No."

"Or do you mean my son Miguel?" He reached for a decanter and poured himself some brandy. "Is that the son? Miguel, who wanted to be a great painter? Who loved Velásquez and Delacroix, Tamayo and Cuevas? Miguel, who spoke of beauty constantly and the ideal, and would walk alone on the Malecon in the first fogs of the Cuban winter? That son? Are you asking about Miguel, rifle? Miguel, who went off, finally, with a broken heart, crazy with grief and loss and ugliness. That son, who is dead to the world? My second son, in love with beauty? Is that the son you speak of?"

"I mean Pepe."

"Pepe is dead too."

"No, he isn't, old man. He was in this house tonight. I followed him from here. He left in an ambulance and went to a whorehouse and I saw him there."

"Pepe is dead."

"I think I'll kill you."

A nerve twitched in his face, but he did not look at me. He sniffed the brandy.

"He was alive when we were still all together in the old country, but something happened later," Don Luis said. "He was always big and physical, a boy who loved horses and the sea. He sailed boats. He learned to fly a plane. He never bothered with Rafael and he laughed at Miguel. But he was my oldest. He was my heir. And he was the angriest, the most

—ferocious. The most macho. He more than the others killed my wife."

"What do you mean?"

"His hatred for Castro was the most violent. In '58, when Castro was still in the Sierra, he worked against him. He even joined the rebels as a spy. He sucked in Miguel. He . . . I think he drove Rafael to join the Brigade. After we left, he spoke of nothing else. Kill Castro and kill the Revolution. It was his passion, his life. When Rafael went to fight, and did not come back, my wife . . . just gave up. Like a plant too long deprived of water. She knew she would never see Cuba again. And we were living here in Mexico, in a slum, in a building filled with thieves and murderers, and all love was gone, all flowers, all the green of the mountains of Cuba, all the blue of the ocean. I wanted to go to Miami, at least to hear the ocean at night. But Pepe said we must stay. Pepe said we had orders to stay. The Americans said we must stay, and if we stayed, things would be all right. They were giving us a reward. But we knew, Elena and I, that the world had changed, and rewards would make no difference. There would never be a day again when we would walk the Malecon and feel the sea spray on our faces. We knew. But Pepe did not know. Pepe did not accept. Pepe vowed revenge. Pepe was certain he would go back. Pepe was always certain."

He did not stop. He ran down. It was as if all the words had lain within him for a long time, coiled there and waiting for release. And now they were out, and the spring was unwound. He sipped the brandy again.

"What did he do? In his certainty, what exactly did he do?"

"I don't know. Not with any precision. I will never know. I do not want to know."

"But you now have many banks. Where did the first bank come from? If you lived in a slum, how did you get a bank?"

"It was Pepe's bank."

"The pictures and newspaper stories all showed you as the owner."

He laughed bitterly. "Lies. To a camera, I looked like the sort of man who ran a bank. Pepe looked like the sort of man who ran a whorehouse. So I was made the owner. On paper. But it was never mine. From the start, after Miguel . . . went away, it was Pepe's bank."

"But you must have known something."

He reached into a small humidor and took out a cigar. He lit it slowly and said: "I knew that when they brought me papers I signed them. I knew that when a branch was opened, I would pose for the photographers, and look learned for the visiting dignitaries. I knew that when it was time to pay a bribe, a *mordida* to a politician, I delivered it and gave it over at lunch and never mentioned it. I knew how to be silent. I was perfect."

"Why are you telling me these things?"

"Because you have a rifle pointed at my chest."

"No," I said. "It is for more than that. You do not like your son, Pepe, do you?"

He paused. Then:

"No."

"Did you like his first wife?"

He bit the end off the cigar and spat it into the fire. "*Esa puta*," he said.

"She was a *puta* in New York. Was she also a *puta* here?"

"She was the kind of whore who does not present a bill until very much later."

"I've known a few of those myself," I said.

He smiled thinly. "We all have. We usually marry them. I was lucky. But my son wasn't."

"Perhaps they deserved each other, Don Luis."

"Perhaps."

I relaxed and let the rifle lie in my lap. "You are a good man, Don Luis."

"No. Only weak."

He dragged on the cigar, and squashed himself

deeper into the chair, his right hand buried in the pocket of his robe. The aroma of the cigar filled the humid air. And for a moment I tried to be Pepe: on the run, knowing that my phony death was now exposed, that an American was after me, possibly a reporter or an agent or a hoodlum. I had more money than I would ever be able to spend, but I had to get out of Mexico. Mexico was too big to buy. The Americans had too much power here. I could leave my father, who was too old to run, let him take the fall, bribe him out of trouble later. But I would have to go quickly. I would need help. I would need papers . . . Of course . . . I looked at Don Luis and took a wild shot.

"Where do you keep your passport, old man?"

Something moved quickly in his eyes, a moment of fear and calculation and animal alert. He sat there, holding the cigar like a man posing for a portrait.

"I . . . don't remember. Pepe's office, uh, usually . . ."

"You remember," I said, raising the rifle. "Pepe was staying here. This was to be the last stop before he made his break. He could never risk going to his office, where he would be seen. You couldn't go there either, not to look for passports. So it's here. In the house. You keep your passport where Pepe keeps his. And I know he wouldn't have come back here in that ambulance after I saw him tonight."

He blinked. "You talk as if you know us. Perhaps you don't really know us. Perhaps we don't do things the way you imagine we do."

"Perhaps. But I can see in your eyes that I'm right."

He sighed, and flicked an ash onto the floor, and rose slowly. He turned and faced the corridor.

"There's a safe in the bedroom," he said.

"Let's open it, *viejo*."

His slippers made a slapping sound on the tiles as he led the way to the bedroom. I had only glimpsed it earlier, but now it seemed like a room in a museum, the inhabitants long buried. There was a massive Colonial Spanish bed with baroque pillars in all the corners, red plush covering, muted lamps at the sides. A tapestry hung behind the headboard, showing medieval hunters cornering a boar. Small fur rugs were scattered like a chain of islands on the cold tile floor. In a glass-doored bookcase, expensive leather-bound collections of Spanish masters stood in neat rows, like men in cells: prisoner Lorca, prisoner Cervantes, prisoner de Vega.

Don Luis stopped before a large wash drawing that looked like a Tiepolo, and lifted it off the hook. A two-foot square wall safe was underneath, with a recessed dial. I lowered the rifle, staring at the safe.

And Don Luis whirled, a small .25-caliber pistol in his right hand, and fired.

I leaned away, and the bullet made a pinging sound as it rocketed around the room. I chopped at his gun hand with the rifle, and the pistol fell to the floor. I shoved him back onto the bed.

"You son of a bitch," I said. "I should kill you right now."

"Do it," he said, spitting out the words. "You ask me to betray my son."

"He'll betray you first. He already has."

"Well, then, kill me."

I started to let him up, and then heard breathing, and turned to see the outside guard framed in the bedroom doorway, blood running down the front of his face from the skulling I had given him, and a crazy wildness in his eyes. He had a rifle in his hands.

We fired almost simultaneously. The noise was deafening, booming off all that tile, held by those thick walls.

He smiled, gurgled, and pitched forward on his face.

I stood there, frozen, listening for other sounds. I hadn't shot anyone in a long time. Don Luis had a knuckle to his chin, waiting. I walked over and looked at the guard. He was breathing shallowly, and I could see a hole in his lower back. The rifle was under him. He would probably live. The poor dumb son of a bitch.

I walked back across the room and picked up the little pistol and put it in my pocket. Then I turned to Don Luis.

"Now open that safe."

He got up wearily and walked to the dial. A turn to the left, another to the right, another left. It clicked open.

"Don't reach into it," I said. "Go over there and sit down on the floor with your back to the wall and your hands in front of you."

He did what I told him to do. His cigar was smoldering on the tile floor. I picked it up and rolled it to him. He examined it, and then took a drag. I put the rifle down on an end table, and reached into the safe.

There wasn't much, but it was enough to understand some things. There were almost a dozen passports, from at least six countries. At different times in the 1960s, Pepe Fuentes had been a Costa Rican named Rodriguez, a Chilean named Rosario, a Bolivian named Escobar. He had been a Puerto Rican with an American passport and a Guatemalan. There was an old Cuban government passport, dated 1957, showing a lot of traffic to the United States and the Dominican Republic, and a spanking new Mexican passport in the name of Javier Soto Anzures but using Pepe's photograph. There were driver's licenses and credit cards, letters of credit and letters of introduction, all dated within the last six months, all introducing Javier Soto Anzures of Barcelona, Spain. Pepe had prepared himself well for departure and a new life. Another folder was full of official letters: one from the White House, dated October 1959, signed by someone whose name was unreadable. It thanked Pepe Fuentes for the heroism of his recent mission, but did not go into details. Another was on the letterhead of the Central Intelligence Agency. It said simply: "Well done" and was signed with a handwritten

"H". A separate folder contained passports for Mrs.
Soto Anzures and the children. At the bottom I found
a large manila envelope from the New York Bank and
Trust. "Sam Briscoe" was written across the front with
a felt-tipped pen. The handwriting was familiar. I
used to live with the girl who wrote the name out so
hastily before dying.

"Who put this envelope in here?" I said.

"I don't know. It's not my safe. It belongs to my
son."

"But you knew the combination."

"A good valet usually does," he said wearily.

I opened the clasp and spread the contents of
the envelope on the end table. There were Xerox
copies of bank statements, canceled checks, memos,
interoffice correspondence, all signed by Pepe Fuentes.
I was certain that if someone who knew numbers
looked at those sheets they would prove the systematic
looting of the bank's assets; they might have mattered,
even a few days ago, but now they were just history.
So were the other papers: pages ripped from books,
copies of testimony released by the Church Committee, Xerox copies of magazine articles about Cuba
and the C.I.A.: the kind of documents that an amateur
would assemble to build a case. But there was one
more thing: a photograph. I remembered it clearly
because it was that photograph of Anne Fletcher that
was taken in Havana after the victory in 1959, surrounded by *barbudos*, young, laughing, beautiful. She
had circled the head of one of the *barbudos* with a
red felt-tip, and had drawn an arrow and written the
name "Camilo." I recognized him as Camilo Cienfuegos, and I had forgotten how young all of Fidel's
men had been that year of victory. Standing beside
Camilo was another young man. She had circled his
head and pointed an arrow to him too. It was Pepe
Fuentes. And some things began to tumble together.

I turned to Don Luis: "Get up." He put out the
cigar on the floor, like a man who no longer cared
about the place where he lived. I shoveled all the

documents into the manila folder, and picked up the rifle.

"I didn't want you to get a chill down on the floor," I said. "That wouldn't be nice."

"You weren't so considerate of him," he said icily, as we moved around the wounded guard.

"He would have killed me," I said. "I wish I could be sorry, but I'm not."

"The police will make you feel sorry," he said sternly. "This is my house. He works for me. You have broken in." He coughed slightly. "And you might have killed this man."

"The police will do nothing to me," I said, without conviction. "When they see these papers. When they realize who and what Pepe Fuentes was."

The old man chuckled. "You are more naive than I thought. The Mexican police work closely with the Americans. Your Embassy will take one look at those documents, and forget you."

"Maybe," I said. "But maybe not."

The fire was almost out. The old man reached for a poker, looked at me as if for permission, received it, and then started poking the logs into life.

"I can call a doctor, if you like," he said. "If he doesn't die, things will be easier."

"I'll be gone soon," I said. "There are a few more things I have to know."

"I know very little."

"Where is Moya Vargas?" I said.

"That I truly do not know. I know that she was away from Mexico. For a long time. In New York. I know that she has now returned to Mexico. I don't know where she is now. Perhaps in Acapulco."

"Pepe has a house there?"

"The Casa Azul. On the point beyond the Caleta. And a yacht."

"Is Pepe there with her?"

He sighed. "I am tired, young man."

"You are a good man," I said, "but I will still kill you if necessary."

He took a weary drag on the cigar and stared into the fire.

I reached over, holding the rifle like a pistol, and pushed the point of the barrel against his cheekbone. "It will be messy," I said. "You will have a closed coffin at the Cathedral."

His eyes were poised between resignation and hope. They chose hope.

"Don't," he said.

I lowered the rifle. He breathed out hard, but I was more relieved than he was.

"Tell me about the bank," I said. "Maybe then I'll know where to find Pepe."

He made a dry, wheezing sound that might have started out to be a chuckle.

"There is no bank any more. Not here. Not in New York. The money is all gone."

"You mean he looted the bank in Mexico too?"

Don Luis nodded slowly. "Somewhere he has two hundred million dollars that do not belong to him. That is one reason why I do not care about myself. I am too old to run. So I will die. I hope that I do not go to hell. I fear hell. If I did not fear hell I would take pills. But I will die. Soon."

"*All* of the money is gone?"

"Yes."

"Jesus Christ."

"Pepe will run. To some country that is friendly to money. The way Vesco did. To Costa Rica. To Chile. To Brazil. To somewhere. He might even take me, in some sudden attack of sentimentality." He gave a hopeless little wave of the cigar. "But he will never be safe."

"That money belongs to a lot of people."

"Yes, and some of them are not very nice," Don Luis said, dragging more confidently on his cigar.

"What do you mean?"

"They were never . . . what you would call nice. They were from strange places. Never from Mexico. Always from outside. They always came with cash.

Sometimes many suitcases full of cash, in small bills. Sometimes with large bills. But always cash. That is why the bank was successful."

"You mean you were running a laundry?"

He squinted again. "What do you mean, laundry?"

"A place where mob guys bring skimmed money from Vegas, or gambling money, or dope money, any kind of money made illegally. They bring it to a bank, deposit it, leave it for a while, and then make withdrawals in nice fresh new bills."

He leaned forward conspiratorially.

"What did you say your name was?"

"I didn't."

"But you have been around."

"A little."

"Maybe you work for these people who came to our little laundry?"

"No. There have been days when I've considered it, but not for longer than fifteen minutes at a time."

"I believe you," he said. "I have no reason to believe you, but I do."

A ways off, I heard dogs barking again. It was time to go. And I would have to go out the front door.

"There's one more thing," I said. He looked very old and tired now, as if there was nothing left for him to say about anything.

"Yes?"

"The death of Camilo Cienfuegos."

"That . . . that was a mistake."

"Tell me about the mistake."

"It was supposed to be Fidel Castro," he said, in a flat voice. "Pepe worked on it for months, with the American."

"What American?"

"The one with the scar on his cheek. I never knew his name. He ran a record store in Havana, and he gave Pepe his orders. Later he gave us the bank."

"He told Pepe to kill Fidel?"

He nodded yes. "Pepe worked on it for months.

He got himself assigned to the air base at Camaguey. Sooner or later Fidel would be in Camaguey, and the orders were to kill him when the opportunity presented itself. Well, that morning Fidel was supposed to leave from Camaguey after opening a school or something. There was an extra plane at the airport. For Pepe. The flight to Havana would take Fidel out over the sea, and the plan was for Pepe to take off immediately afterwards and shoot Fidel out of the air. That would have been the end of this Communism thing . . ."

"And Fidel didn't take the plane."

"He went back to Havana by car. Camilo Cienfuegos was on the plane."

"And Pepe shot it down on schedule."

His jaw twitched, but he never answered. He was looking past me.

I turned, and something high and white exploded in my skull, and I lurched sideways, and caught a glimpse of Moya Vargas, and then was smashed again, and spun away into a great dark tunnel, where a pinprick of light shone in the distance, then disappeared.

19

I was awake and freezing, but I still could see nothing in the world. My face was pressing in muck and I couldn't move my arms and legs. I was naked. A dirty blossom opened and closed inside my skull. I listened, and heard the wind combing the trees, and the murmur of voices, speaking musical Spanish somewhere outside. I turned over, and reached my handcuffed hands to the side of my head. I felt a broad soft pulpy area above my right ear. The blossom opened again and stayed open. Someone had hit me with a board or a rifle or a club. Someone who was with Moya Vargas. It had to be someone else, not Moya, because I remembered seeing her hard handsome face, and she was in the wrong position to hit me, too far over to the right. They must have come in that back door, through the laundry room, walking softly past the bound guard, probably barefoot, padding along the carpets and the tile. I wondered where Don Luis was now.

Slowly my eyes adjusted and I could see long bright vertical lines in the blackness. Places where the boards of a wall did not properly join. I rolled over in the muck, smelling old dung, the dried lather of horses, a deeper, loamier animal smell, and something else that must have been hay. I was in a barn. I rolled again, until I reached the vertical cracks.

Outside, in a moonlit clearing, two Mexicans stood beside a well, pouring gasoline from tin drums over Murray's car. There were a few scrubby trees in the clearing, which ended at a cliff. In the moonlight I could not tell how far it was to the bottom of the cliff. I was sure it must be far enough to kill any-one in a car and make a flaming crash convincing. I tried to stand up but the cuffs dug into my ankles. I shuddered in the cold.

Then I heard a car in the distance, grinding its way up a hill trail. The two Mexicans turned to look at the lights, and a Pontiac station wagon pulled around past a screen of trees into the clearing. Moya Vargas got out on the passenger side, swinging a can-vas handbag. She was wearing a black jump suit with a long zipper down the front, and her hair was piled high in a severe bun. She looked over at the barn, and said something to the Mexicans. She looked hard and quick and invulnerable.

Then the driver got out. It took him a long time. He was large and running to fat. It was the agent who had followed me around New York. The man I had left naked in the snow in front of the Elizabeth Street station house. He opened the back of the sta-tion wagon and removed the gallon drums of gasoline. Then he and Moya went over and talked to the two Mexicans. I couldn't hear what they said. They looked in my direction. Then Moya said something else to the Mexicans. One of the Mexicans laughed. I could hear dogs barking. In Mexico, the dogs were always bark-ing. They strolled closer to the barn, as the Mexicans lifted the cans and walked to Murray's car.

"I don't know why we're wasting time here with this bum," the fat guy said. "Pepe is liable to take off."

"Not while I have those passports," she said. "He can't go anywhere without them. And I've got them."

"You mean *we've* got them."

"Yes, Lloyd," she said, in an amused way. "*We've* got them."

"What did he say when you talked to him?"

"I told you that before, Lloyd. He said he'd wait."

"Did he say anyone else was coming?"

"You mean from the agency?"

"I mean anyone else period."

"He didn't say."

"They could just wait for us down there and whack us out," Lloyd said. There was a whine in his voice, like a kid who was about to play hooky and didn't really want to do it.

"You worry too much, Lloyd."

"Well, why would Pepe let us live? He's got some boys down there in Acapulco. We could end up a free lunch for the sharks."

I could hear her chuckle, they were that close to the barn now.

"I told Pepe you were with me," she said. "I said we had some other help. I told him that if he tried to play funny he would never leave Acapulco alive. As it was, I told him, he was lucky we were only asking for half."

"Wud he say?"

"He said he would wait."

"And you believe him?"

"I know him, Lloyd. I was married to him." A pause. "He'll wait." Another pause. "And he'll split with us."

Lloyd spat. Then: "I don't know why we just don't shoot this bum in the barn."

"He's a newspaperman, that's why," she said. "He has friends all over New York. If he's shot, they'll come looking. Every newspaperman in Mexico City will come looking too. We don't know what he knows, who he's talked to."

"I'd like to put a bullet through his head."

"You take things too personally, Lloyd," she said. "If you hadn't been so clumsy with that Carter girl, he'd be in jail. He'd never have seen Pepe. He'd never have talked to Don Luis."

"I did it my way," he said. "The Carter broad was flaky. She liked this bum. She said she couldn't set him up, she wanted to go home. When I said she'd have to go through with the deal, she said she'd tell Briscoe everything. I did what I had to do. Besides, she was *yours*, not mine. If I'd'a got someone from the agency, it wouldn'tve worked out this way."

"Now, poor little boy, you'll just have to get rich."

"I just don't like it. I don't like a fake accident. I don't like these two Mexicans. And I don't like what's coming in Acapulco either."

"You'll like the money, Lloyd. How long have you been with the agency, twenty years? Don't you think they owe you something?"

"The way things are going, these investigations, these goddamn reporters, yeah, I feel they owe. Someone owes."

"So do it my way."

"He'll wait for us?"

"He'll wait."

Moya and her fat friend looked at the barn again and then started walking toward me. Moya was leading the way. A gun bulged on the fat man's hip. She had her hands jammed in her pockets, the handbag looped over her forearm.

I rolled over on my side. I heard a board lifted out of lugs on the outside of the barn. Then I saw a shaft of moonlight fall into the barn, as the door scraped open.

"Is he still out?" she said. Her voice had that husky purr it had that night in Brooklyn Heights, a couple of hundred years earlier, but there was a harder edge to it now.

"Let's find out," Lloyd said, a little too eagerly.

I heard his heavy feet squishing in the damp earth as he came for me. I felt cold and small, like a little boy without a blanket.

"Don't kick him," she said toughly. "We don't want too many marks on him, Lloyd."

"I'd like to drop him in that fucking well."

"Such language," she said.

"Fuck you, Moya."

He turned me over with the toe of his shoe. I faked a groan.

"Well," she said, "he's alive. I thought you might have killed him with that rifle butt."

"I wanted to."

"Did you have to strip him?"

"I had my reasons."

"Well, listen to *her!*"

"Not that reason," he snapped. "Other reasons."

I groaned again. She said: "Get some water."

He squished out obediently. Far away, and very high, an airplane droned through the sky. "Briscoe?" she said. I didn't answer.

I heard Lloyd coming back. Water sloshed in a pail. "He's out, all right," Moya said. "Maybe you damaged his brain."

Lloyd grunted, and then poured the water on my face. It was icy and shocking. I blinked awake. They were standing over me. In the shaft of moonlight, I could see her eyes, as old as tombs, looking at me in a cool appraising way.

"Hello, Briscoe," she said.

I tried to smile. "Well, well," I said. "The Latin Bombshell. Straight from a glorious tour of New York. How are you, Moya? Who's the pansy?"

Lloyd kicked me high in the ribs. Pain knifed through my chest. "Jesus," I said, spitting, "you're a brave son of a bitch."

"I'll stomp you out in a minute, Briscoe. I don't really give a shit how you die, you know. And you're gonna die, boy. You better believe it. You're gonna die . . ."

"Stop it, will you, Lloyd?" she said, in an exasperated way. "If you kill him now, we'll never find out anything."

"And if I die, I'll never find out anything either," I said.

"See? He's a wise-ass, Moya. I'd like to break his goddamned head, this wise-ass."

"Go outside, will you?" she said sharply.

"I don't have to take orders from you," he said.

"Oh yes, you do, boy!"

It suddenly hit me: maybe this guy really *was* gay.

He turned and stomped out. She watched him go, and then went over to the barn door, and closed it most of the way, shifting her bag to her shoulder. She stood over me, looking at me. All of me. For what seemed like a long time.

"He's very nice," I said.

"Don't be funny, Briscoe."

"I have no choice, do I? You're getting ready to cremate me in that automobile out there, so what the hell."

She folded her arms under her breasts and smiled in a cruelly subtle way. "You don't have to go that way, you know."

"If I didn't hurt so much, lady, I'd really laugh."

"What happens to you depends on how you co-operate, Briscoe. It's important that I know everything that you know. Particularly why you're here."

"Sorry, Moya. I got such a bad headache I can't remember anything."

She squatted, putting the handbag on the mucky earth beside her. Her eyes ran up and down my body. She touched my chest with a long coral-painted nail and let it drift down my belly. I could smell something coming off her, a drowsy ripening odor. Her face became more languid. The tip of her tongue moved along the rim of her upper lip.

"I could make you feel good," she said.

"Yeah, I guess you could. You could make me feel better if you took these cuffs off and got me between silk sheets."

"What's this?"

"I was born with it."

Her hand was warm.

"You look like you've used it a lot," she said.

"From time to time."

"Does it get bigger?"

"Usually."

She moved out of my line of vision, and then suddenly my penis was engulfed. Her mouth was hot and tight, her tongue moving quickly in the center of the hotness. All the rest of me was cold. Her hand cupped my testicles. I started to get hard.

"The handcuffs," I whispered. "Take the handcuffs off . . ."

She said nothing. She couldn't.

"I want to touch you," I lied.

And then she pulled away, and unzippered the jump suit and stepped out of it, leaving her boots on. She was naked underneath. The moon threw blue highlights through her hair. I tried to see what was happening in the yard, but the door was only at an angle to the moon. The cars and the well were out of sight to the left.

"I'm going to fuck you real good," she said, growling in a theatrical way, "and then we'll talk."

She stood over me, straddling me, a leg on either side, and squatted again, reaching under herself to hold me with her coral-painted nails and then sliding slowly onto my penis. I reached up with my cuffed hands and played delicately with her nipples. She reached down, and put one hand on her clitoris and the other on my throat. Up and down. Her eyes growing wide and unfocussed. Up and down. She tossed her head, but the bun stayed in place. Up and down. Still squatting in her boots, so that her knees would not get dirty. Tight and wet and smelling of musk. Engulfing the full shaft. Raping me.

Until her hand began moving faster and faster, in steady pulsing circular movements and I felt her move down harder on me in a spreading jamming thrusting movement and I pinched her nipples with

my thumb and forefinger and she leaned back, biting
her lower lip, trying to smother the sound of orgasm.

And I reached over quickly to the purse and
fumbled with my cuffed hands for the gun that I knew
was lying inside.

Grabbed it.

And jammed it into her taut belly.

"Stop right there, sweetheart," I said. "Or you'll
never come again."

Her eyes were wide with fear. I felt like laughing
out loud.

"Put that down," she said, a muzzy formlessness
in her voice.

"Not until I put a bigger hole in your belly than
anyone can have and live."

"You son of a bitch."

"Just reach into that bag and get the key to
these cuffs, Moya."

I sat up, keeping the .45 jammed into her belly.

"I don't have the keys," she said.

"Who does?"

"Lloyd."

"Call him in here."

She shrugged. I was sticky with her.

"Lloyd?" she shouted. "Come in here."

I listened, but couldn't hear his heavy feet.

"Where is he?"

"Right here, Briscoe."

I turned, and Lloyd fired from the darkness. I
rolled and fired at the muzzle blast. He fired again, the
bullet thumping into the muck, and this time I aimed.
The .45 was very loud. He didn't say a word, or make
a sound, but I heard him fall heavily in the darkness.

When I turned around Moya was gone, and so
was her jump suit.

The key was on a ring in Lloyd's jacket pocket. I
clamped the key in my teeth, and after four tries,

got it into the lock between my wrists. I turned my
hands and the cuffs clicked open. Then I opened the
cuffs on my ankles. My arms and legs were numb and
I rubbed them briskly to get the blood flowing again.
I couldn't see Lloyd, but I could hear his strangled
breathing. I faded deeper into the barn, still naked
and very cold, holding the .45. I heard an engine
start and through one of the cracks I saw the station
wagon, jerking around in reverse, starting to leave.
One of the Mexicans was running away from the
front of the barn, and the second was behind the
wheel, shouting and holding the door open. Moya
was probably in the station wagon too but I couldn't
see her. I moved to the door, to take a shot at them.
Try to hit a wheel. Try to hit a driver.

Then one of the Mexicans lit a match and threw
it to the ground and the earth around him erupted
into fire. A long trail of blazing gasoline ran straight
at the barn. I stepped out the door into a wall of
flame, and ducked back inside. I moved along the
walls, looking for another door. The walls of the barn
were burning now, the wood crackling loudly. Then
I stumbled over Lloyd, lying on his side in the dark,
not moving, and fell against a pile of farm tools
stacked against a back wall. Above them was a window screened with chicken wire nailed to the frame.
I grabbed a pitchfork, jammed it into the chicken
wire and twisted hard, pulling it away from the nails.
Then I smashed at the frame. The fire was in the
barn now, licking at the walls, driving into the piles
of damp straw, turning it to smoke. I went to Lloyd
and saw his .45 lying beside him. I picked it up,
threw both guns out the open window, and climbed
out after them. Maybe Lloyd was still alive, but I
wasn't going back in there to find out.

I picked up the guns and sprinted across the
clearing, expecting to hear rifle shots. All I heard
was the distant barking of the goddamned dogs.

All of them were gone. The station wagon had

left, carrying away Moya Vargas and her two burly
servants. In the distance I could see the dull glow in
the sky over Mexico City. The city was at least a
thousand feet below me. At that height, I knew I
must be somewhere out past Toluca. I looked at
Murray's car, which was glistening with gasoline. My
clothes were draped over a low branch of one of the
scrawny trees.

Behind me the barn sighed, blew out at the sides,
and then collapsed. I had to move quickly. These
hills were inhabited, and someone was certain to
come along soon. I went to the well, drew a pail of
water, and washed the worst of the barn muck off my
body. Then I did it again. I felt better, but my hair
would need a shower or a stream. Still wet, I started
pulling on my clothes while I walked to the edge of
the cliff. It was a sheer drop of at least 400 feet. I
shivered, but not from the cold.

I went back to the car, left the door open and
sat on the edge of the seat. For a long moment, I
hesitated about starting the engine. A spark from the
ignition could turn the car into a torch. I put one foot
on the accelerator and the other on the ground, ready
to sprint away if there was an explosion. And turned
the key.

The engine started.

And there was no explosion.

I slammed the door, breathing hard, laid the two
.45s on the seat beside me, and drove down the
mountain. The road was dirt for the first 300 yards
and then became a single-lane blacktop. Three Mexican farmers in white pajamas, carrying machetes,
were hurrying up the road. I yelled at them.

"Back there! *Bandidos! Cuidado, hombres! Bandidos!*"

They looked at me blankly, glanced up the mountain, and stepped aside as I hurried past them. At the
bottom of the blacktop I hit the main road. The road
sloped off to the left to descend the mountain, climbed

to the right to go over it. I was sure the cops would be coming up the mountain. Cops everywhere don't like working in the cold. I turned right, heading over the mountain. Some of the high distant slopes were topped with snow.

I passed a few trucks, groaning under loads of steel rod and concrete blocks. I was very hungry. A station wagon full of tourists came by on the other side of the road. Their car had California plates. They were laughing as they whizzed by. After fifteen minutes, I reached the crest of the mountain. I was nauseated from the smell of gasoline. The gas gauge was on empty, so I coasted down the mountain, lightly riding the brake. In the distance I saw a few lights. A woodcutter, with tinder strapped in a neat stack to his back, walked by and waved. The lights got larger, and then I turned and found myself at a tiny crossroads: a gas station, a cantina, a few obscure houses. I needed gas, and for the first time realized that my wallet and passport were gone. I groped in my pockets and found a small roll of pesos. About 300 pesos. Not really enough. But enough. I pulled into the station and told the attendant to fill the tank while I went next door to the cantina. The cantina was almost empty. Two woodcutters sat at a table, drinking morosely. I ordered a cold Carta Blanca and some crackers and paid six pesos. My body was sore. I thanked the barman and wished him a very *buenas noches.* I opened the trunk and all of my things were still there, even the tape recorder. The gas station attendant looked at me blankly and asked about the smell of gasoline on the car. It was because of a mistake, I told him. Some *bobo* had started to wash the car with gasoline instead of water. Ah, he said. The world is full of *bobos.* Yes, I said, and paid him and went on.

I drove another sixty miles until I reached a town called Tlaloc. Named for the rain god. There was a vile little motel at the edge of town. I pulled in, paid

eighty pesos cash in advance, parked the car, unloaded
the suitcase, and was sent to a little cottage near the
back of a filthy courtyard. I undressed, put the two
.45s under the pillow, and lay down to sleep.

I was in a lot of trouble now. The Mexico City
cops were after me for killing a girl I hardly knew. I
might have really killed the guard at the house of
Don Luis, and I had probably killed Lloyd, who
worked for my own government. So I couldn't go to
the cops for help and I couldn't go to the American
Embassy. But I had seen enough and heard enough
now to be sure that Anne Fletcher had probably been
murdered by one of Pepe's people, that Moya understood immediately and left New York to cut herself
into one of the biggest jackpots in history. She knew
Pepe was alive, and she knew where to find him. She
must have called one of Pepe's old fellow workers for
help the moment I left her apartment, and so Lloyd
ended up tracking me and wandering on my roof, and
when that got messed up, she told him to send the
Carter girl on whatever plane I took to Mexico City.
She was as close to an innocent bystander as anyone
in this thing. I knew that if the old man survived the
next few days, I could probably prove that the Fuentes
family had been given a bank in Mexico by the C.I.A.
as a reward for killing one of the highest-ranking
members of the Cuban government, during a time
when we still had diplomatic relations; that the bank
was essentially a laundry, used by mob guys and C.I.A.
types; that it had expanded into the United States,
and had then been looted. It was a hell of a story.
All I had to do was prove it.

I lay there for a while in the strange room, in
that town I'd never heard of, with no money, in a
dangerous country that was not my own. On the wall
there was a cheap Rivera print of a peasant woman
carrying water on her shoulder, and there were stains
in the plaster underneath. I remembered my room at
the Geneva, with the lights of Mexico City blinking

outside in the night, and I thought about the dead.

On the way to unconsciousness, I prayed to Tla-loc. A little rain would be nice for the car. I knew it wouldn't do a goddamn thing for me.

20

I woke to the pounding of the rain. It was hammering on the rooftop of the cottage, lashing the windows, attacking the morning with a long deep drumming roar. I thanked Tlaloc. He was my kind of god. Prompt and generous. I got up and tried to see out of the window, but there was only a gray blur. I went into the shower and picked up a tiny sliver of green Palmolive soap. I used all of it, standing under the hot water, but I couldn't seem to wash the smell of Moya Vargas off my body.

I smelled her as I brushed away the caked mud from my slacks and jacket. I smelled her as I dressed, and looked at the guns and checked the clips. I smelled her as I opened the door, and said one little thank-you prayer to Tlaloc. I had about a hundred pesos left. I went to the motel office, staying under the tin roof of the overhang, and broke the 100-peso bill. Then I went into the restaurant and paid ten pesos for *huevos rancheros* and coffee. I ate greedily. The rain pounded down.

After breakfast I ran through the rain to the car. The outside was clean, but the smell of gasoline clung to the interior. I wasn't sure where I was. I opened the glove compartment to look for maps, and my wallet and passport fell out on the floor. Of course. They would not have wheeled me off a cliff without leaving some identification. This way it would all be very neat. The American who killed a girl in the Hotel Geneva was found drunk and burned to death at the bottom of a cliff on a road in the mountains. I looked in the wallet. Almost $800, in American and Mexican money. In the glove compartment the wallet might have survived the fire, and the local Mexican cops could have pocketed the bills and shrugged away the death. What the hell was $800 if you had $100 million waiting over the mountains? The passport was intact. I poked deeper into the glove compartment and found a pint of Bacardi rum. Murray, I thought, you are the complete car owner. I opened the bottle and took a belt and then looked at the maps.

The town of Tlaloc was not more than a dozen miles from the main road to San Miguel Allende. I could go back to Mexico City, but Moya had probably tipped the cops. They would be checking the planes leaving Mexico City for Acapulco, trying to find the gringo killer of the red-haired girl. But the map showed I could go another way. Through San Miguel to Guanajuato. And in San Miguel I could find the bearded artist who had cried at the death of his brother. Michael Fountain. Miguel Fuentes. He was alive. Maybe he was ready to tell his story. If he was, maybe I could prove what I already knew. As I drove slowly through the storm, and then out of it, I felt as if I were in some other century, in a Mexico before the revolutions and the betrayals of the revolutions. This was the Mexico where the *mestizo* worked for the *hacendado* from birth until death. Nothing was changed; the land least of all. And I remembered how Mexico had felt to me long ago, when I was young, how it was a kind of hospital of the spirit for me, a place that rebarbarized the healthy parts of the soul, and let you shuck off the rest. I always thought of boots on rock when I thought of Mexico, not soft slippers for cars and living rooms and restaurants. Boots on rock and men with leather skin standing on hillsides, with machetes in their hands. That was Mexico to me.

And here they were, as I drove the road to Queretaro, those old men at the side of the road, toothless and womanless, with the landscape of fields and mountains spread out behind them. In that old photograph, Camilo Cienfuegos had been so young;

he was not yet thirty; all of them were young then, my age then, Fidel, Che, Camilo. Even Pepe was young. The game of What If was a foolish one to play in the real world. But if Pepe had succeeded in his mission that day, if he had killed Fidel, history might have been different. There would have been no Bay of Pigs. No missile crisis. Maybe not even a Lee Harvey Oswald. And maybe then, no Vietnam, no Johnson, no Nixon, no Watergate. Anne Fletcher would be alive, and Nicola Carter, and poor dumb Lloyd, and that guard who went to work for the wrong family in Las Lomas. And I would not be driving on this road in Mexico, trying to find a man I'd never met. Traffic picked up as I passed the mountains, and I found the main road. Buses and trucks spewed filth into the air of the valley. There were a lot of Renaults and Volkswagens, and then the entrance to a super highway going north where you paid a fifteen-peso toll. I stayed within the speed limit, but nobody else did. They roared past me, honking in macho contempt for my sloth or timidity. And then as I moved further north, the road began to empty and the smog from the central valley began to clear and the sun splashed on the long lava-smooth slopes of the mountains.

The super highway ended, the four-lane road became a two-lane road, and I passed through villages where short blocky women washed clothes at stone sinks and boys played soccer in the dusty yards. I came out of one village, picked up speed and saw a dead dog ahead of me, his guts strandy and red against the tar. A bus was coming straight at me in the other lane, so I had to bump over the dog. My head ached.

There were green fields and then fields splashed with orange as if some mad pointillist giant had started work that morning and decided to go home for lunch. I moved through Queretaro, and out on to another two-lane road, and then ahead I saw the sign for San Miguel de Allende.

I turned left onto a road made of tezontle stone, dark and red in the clean light of the countryside. The road was very straight. Over in a wooded grove, a colonial church stood like a challenge from the old order. A car behind me honked, accelerated and passed me, scattering a herd of goats walking with a shepherd boy on the other side of the road. I knew that I might have to do some ugly things in the next few days. But out on that road, I wanted to savor it all, the perfect day, the scrubbed sky, the endless fields, the distant dead volcanoes.

Up ahead, I saw a country bus stop, a huge lumbering Flecha del Norte bus pulling out in a swirl of dust, and a small boy running from behind a building. The boy's suitcase was dragging him back, and the bus threw out its poisoned cloud and left. The boy was too late. In silhouette, I saw him punch his thigh in anger and disappointment.

I pulled into the dusty clearing beside the bus stop. The boy was about fifteen, wearing a cheap suit, carrying a rough suitcase tied around the outside with rope.

I opened the door.

"*Rapidamente, chico!*" I said.

He looked at me, suspicious. And then jumped in.

I gunned the engine, and hurled the car down the highway in pursuit of the bus. The boy smiled. And then laughed. The bus was doing seventy. I looked in the rearview mirror. No cops. No cars. No anything. Just the ribbon of red road slicing through the land behind us. And I started laughing too. Driving like some dumb high school kid.

I honked the horn furiously as we passed the bus, and the boy waved frantically with his arms, and pointed to the side of the road. And slowly the bus began to drift back, and finally pulled over. I slowed as the bus slowed, and pulled over and let the kid out.

"Muchissimas gracias, señor," he said. He seemed astonished.

"Por nada."

He ran back to the bus.

I hit the gas and roared on, down the tezontle stone road. Five minutes later, I came to an open space in the side of the road, made a long wide turn, and then shockingly, suddenly, San Miguel was there, lying below me in the sun.

It was almost too beautiful: a town of houses huddled against hills, with church steeples pointing like fingers at the sky, tiled rooftops, cobblestoned streets, men in straw hats, swaybacked women carrying water jugs; a town off the travel posters; a town that I used to think was Mexico, years ago, before I knew anything about Mexico or the world.

One street led into the town, but there was a truck sliding uneasily down one side of the street while a bus groaned up the steep angle on the other. So I waited helplessly behind the truck while a young boy on a mule clopped by on the narrow strip of sidewalk. Finally the bus passed the truck, and traffic moved again, and I went all the way down the hill riding the brake, until I could go no farther, and then turned left, and right and left again into a main street, along the main street and into the Zocalo.

I drove slowly past the Zocalo, looking for a hotel, and went past a lot of jewelry and trinket shops, and out to a broader street, where more trucks wheezed and heaved their way to some other place in Mexico. I saw a large official-style building on my left, and behind a fence on my right a hotel, painted white, was lying in the sun. It was called the Posada de Aldea. As I turned through its gates, I realized that the large official building was the Art Institute. I looked at my watch. It was eleven in the morning. Good. I could check in, wash, eat some lunch and then go out and explore the town on foot. I parked the car in a lot behind the main building.

The hotel had a wide, airy lobby. A man was on his knees, polishing the tile floor by hand. He did not look up. A young girl was behind the desk. She gave me a big smile. She was Mexican and quite young.

"How long you stay, *señor?*" she said.

"I don't know," I said. "I'm going to check out the Institute."

"Ah yes, across the street. We have special rates for students, if you stay long. Please do not forget to ask the special rates, okay?"

"Okay."

She smiled, and handed me a key, and a man went out and got my bag and my typewriter.

"Oh, you are a writer, yes?"

"Most of the time," I said.

"Well, write something good here."

"I'll try."

I ordered a sandwich, soup and tea from room service and then opened the suitcase and laid out some clean clothes. I stepped into the shower, and tried again to scour Moya Vargas off my body. When I got out of the shower, the sandwich was on a tray on the bureau. The tile floors felt cool on my bare feet. I ate the sandwich. It was more bread than ham. But the soup was good and the tea was marvelous. The clean clothes felt good against my body. I opened the window, which overlooked a small garden. The breeze was cool and clear. At one o'clock I went out.

I walked across the street to the institute. The classrooms were grouped around a large central patio filled with flowers, plants and sculptures. I smelled turpentine and linseed oil, and some other smell that must have come from the fixative sprays that were used to protect chalk drawings. There was an office to the right, and a bulletin board outside, offering rides to Texas and California, houses for sublet, cats, dogs, and furniture. Groups of students talked in the patio, the sound of an instructor's voice droned from some classroom, and the leather huaraches shuffled on stone as the young Americans moved around, playing at their one year of being someone else. A few of them even held hands. I didn't mind them. There was, after all, nothing to mind. And once, years ago, that year on the GI Bill at Mexico City College, I had been like them. Most of them even looked the way we did, sporting beards, and longish hair, and Oaxaca sweaters, carrying Dostoievski and Hemingway, talking in the snatches I could hear about films and bullfights and D. H. Lawrence. Some of them looked lost and some of them looked earnest. Most were on their year in Mexico, and it could do them no real harm, unless they got into trouble with the cops, and either way, they would remember it the rest of their lives. It just wasn't very real. It's never very real when somebody else is paying the bills.

I went into the office. A bright-eyed blonde girl with lank hair and bony shoulders looked up from a card file.

"Yes?"

"I'd like a catalogue."

"Over there," she said curtly. There was a pile of catalogues on the counter to the right. I picked one up, and leafed through it.

"Uh, I'm looking for a friend from New York, a painter named Michael Fountain."

"I'm sorry. We're not an information service, sir."

"Well, I thought he might be teaching here."

"There's nobody by that name teaching here." She went back to the files.

"Excuse me," I said, "I don't really want to be a prick, but I'd like to find out something."

"When you use that kind of language, I don't have to answer you about anything, mister. Good afternoon."

"Hey! I came all the way from New York to find this guy and . . ."

"I don't care if you came from the North Pole, mister."

Spunky woman.

I walked back to the patio holding my catalogue. There was a cafeteria on the far side of the patio, with a supply store beside it. I went into the supply store. There were Windsor and Newton watercolors and a lot of Grumbacher oil paints and piles of cheap Mexican sketchbooks, with each sheet of drawing paper separated by tracing paper, for instructors to mark corrections. The man at the cash register was Mexican. I picked up a sketchbook and some 4B charcoal pencils and went over to pay for them. While he added them up, I asked him some questions.

"Pardon," I said in Spanish, "but I'm looking for a friend. An American."

"*Un Americano?*"

"It's possible that he is American. But it is also possible that he speaks Spanish like a Cuban."

He blinked. "Fourteen pesos, *señor.*"

I counted out twenty pesos. "He is a painter. He is large and bearded. His name is Michael Fountain."

"Fountain."

"*Sí, Fountain. Como Fuente.*"

The mask broke. He smiled, knowing exactly who I meant. "*Ah, sí, Fountain. El borracho.*"

"Yes," I said, smiling, "he drinks a little. Is he in town?"

"He was in San Miguel yesterday, *señor.* Today, who knows? They come and go."

"How long has he been here?"

"Seven, eight years. A long time. He is Cubano?"

"No," I lied. "He speaks with a Cuban accent. That is where he learned Spanish. We were friends in Havana, before Fidel."

"Ah."

"Where does he drink?"

"In the Zocalo. It's where all the Americanos drink."

"And if he is not there?"

"He has a house. *Una casa chica.* With a woman.

A Mexican woman. Over on Cinco de Mayo Street. It's colored yellow."

"*Gracias, amigo.*"

"*Por nada.*"

He smiled, and I slipped him a twenty-peso note. He kept on smiling.

Michael Fountain wasn't in any of the bars on the Zocalo, and it was too early in the day to look for the casa chica that was colored yellow. So I went over to the park and sat on a bench and pretended to draw in the sketchbook. Eventually, if what Murray and the art store man said was true, he would come to the square and its bars.

I doodled in the sketchbook, drawing faces, remembering that year I had wanted to be a painter, and how hard I had worked until I realized I was no good at it. I looked around the square at the things I would sketch if I were an artist. At the four cops lounging in front of the police station, one of them with a rifle slung over his shoulder, watching a fifth cop angle away to the corner to grab a drunken old man and lead him back to the station house for the day's Big Collar. Or the tour bus, pulling around the corner into the Zocalo, and discharging its cargo of sunburned aging Protestants, its men in wash 'n' wear suits and Bermuda shorts and its women with straw bags and sensible shoes. I would draw them. I would draw that old man reading *Novedades* in front of one of the four fountains, the single tame stream coming from each fountain with the force of a small boy pissing while lying on his back. I would show that retired couple, his face tan from the sun, hers still pale under the broad-brimmed hat, walking into the place called Los Dragones de la Reina, the name painted in old English letters, where they examined the brasswork and the antiques. I would try to capture the sense that some tourists always give you, in every country on the earth, that they are sniffing: sniffing for signs of corruption; sniffing for disease;

sniffing for proof of inferiority; sniffing for evidence of incompetence; I would have drawn that sense, if I were any good at all. And added that man in the checkered sport shirt stepping into the Super Tienda to buy a loaf of bread, and the three different shades of pink on the houses that faced the plaza, and the kids climbing on the iron railings of the bandstand in the center, and the birds rushing into the great manicured trees that shaded the square, and the green cab with a Bardahl sign on its roof, circling the square and pointing out buildings to its passengers, and always and inevitably, and in this case standing in the doorway of the shop called the Posada del San Francisco, the man selling a blanket. I was looking at all of these things, and thinking about how to draw them, about their shape and their weight on the page, their relationships and their forms and what is sometimes called their volume, when I looked up and Michael Fountain walked around the corner.

He went past the English-language bookstore, nodded at the shoeshine boys, and kept walking under the arcades. He looked heavy and soggy in a thick Oaxaca sweater. His beard was matted, his head covered with a flat peasant straw hat. He went into a place called La Cucaracha.

I sketched one final picture and then got up and walked over from the park to the arcades and into La Cucaracha.

There were three art students sitting at a corner table, the large brown envelopes that contained their sketchbooks stacked against the wall behind them. They were drinking tequila, and going through the whole elaborate ritual with the salt and the lime. They were very young.

Michael Fountain looked very old. He was sitting alone against the wall, with a Bacardi bottle in front of him. His face was late Hemingway: the gray beard hiding a weak chin, the eyes soft and haunted. He had one leg crossed over another. Small pink hands jutted out of the heavy wool of the sweater. I knew he was about forty-five; he looked sixty.

"Hello, Miguel," I said.

He looked up. Fear scribbled through his eyes, and doubt, and then relief. A smile moved slowly across his face, like a stain.

"I knew you would come for me, sooner or later," he said, in flawless English. His voice was soft, full of an almost sweet acceptance. "Would you like a drink?"

I hadn't expected that. I sat down. "Of course," I said. "Bacardi is fine."

He turned to the barman. "*Oye, Paolito. Traiga otra vaso, por favor.*"

"*Sí, señor.*"

He looked at me as if his life had just entered its final stage. "Are you going to take me away?"

"I'm not a cop, Miguel."

"Then you're with the agency, I suppose."

"No," I said. "I'm a reporter."

"Aw, shit . . ."

The barman brought the glass. I poured myself a half glass of rum from Fountain's bottle.

"You're safer with me than you are with them," I said.

"I'm not interested in safety."

"Then maybe you should try truth."

His eyes blazed. "What truth? Your truth? The agency's truth? Washington's truth? Who the hell wants to hear the truth? Who?"

"I do."

The fire in his eyes died away. "Shit," he said. "Shit."

Two cops in baby-blue uniforms strolled by, glanced in, and kept walking. They were like kids in costumes, out for a walk, except for the rifles.

"I told some people I was coming here to see you," I lied. "They know who you are. They know what you're involved in. You might as well tell me all of it. I have a tape recorder back at the hotel. What you tell me might keep the both of us alive."

He looked at me from out of the soft hunted eyes, and reached for the bottle.

21

We took a cab to the hotel, where I picked up the tape recorder, extra tapes and batteries and some cigarettes, and then we went to the house that was colored yellow. A small bony girl answered Fountain's knock. She wore a thin red dress and he introduced her as Miranda.

"I found her in the street in Guanajuato," he said in English. "She was fifteen and had come from the country and didn't know what she was doing in the city. She still doesn't, and she isn't fifteen anymore, but I love her." He laughed darkly. "If it's possible to use that word about anything or anyone."

"Sometimes it is."

"Maybe it isn't," Fountain said, and led the way into the small two-story house. On the first floor I could see a living room, a bathroom, a kitchen, and an eating area. A back door led out to yards, and I could see open fields and terraced gardens. The living room walls were covered with paintings and drawings, some framed, others on stretched canvas. Some were small lyrical landscapes, mountains crowned by snow, or a lone cactus framed by desert, or clouds rushing across endless fields, heavy with weather. But there was a series of other pictures, most of them self-portraits, in a variety of styles, and they were tortured, anguished, writhing with jagged brushstrokes, raw, livid colors, some squeezed directly from the tubes, faces that snarled and grimaced and cowered. They were like an autobiography in paint. Fountain did not look at them.

"We'll go up to the studio," he said. And then, to Miranda, in Spanish: "Miranda, sweetheart, bring

some rum, some glasses, and some ice." He smiled at
her. "And perhaps some olives." She nodded but did
not smile.

He led the way up the stairs.

The studio filled the entire top floor, and it was
a shambles. An easel dominated the far end of the
room, where the hard afternoon light streamed in with
cruel clarity. On the easel there was a canvas, sized,
tinted a light sienna, but otherwise untouched. A
ceramic-topped kitchen table served as a palette, its
top scabrous with great globs of dried acrylic paint.
There were mounds of newspapers and magazines in
English and Spanish, old coffee cans filled with
rusting water, brushes jammed into vases, stacks of
canvases facing the wall. He moved to a couch against
the far wall. It was covered with stacks of newspapers, flaking and yellowed. Fountain lifted the stack
and dumped them on the floor, and then gestured at
a director's chair, smeared with old paint.

"Pull up a chair."

"This is quite a place."

"There is nothing sadder than the studio of a
painter who no longer paints," he said in Spanish.
"Occasionally I come up here, to visit what I might
have been."

"I wish I had a violin," I said. "I could set that to
music."

He ignored this and looked at the tape recorder.
"Is that thing on?"

"No."

"Miranda!"

She came up the stairs. Something nervous was
happening to her eyes, but I didn't know what it was.
She was carrying a tray with ice, rum, glasses and a
bowl of olives. Her eyes moved around the rubble of
the studio.

"She usually isn't allowed up here," Fountain
said in English. "Today's an occasion."

"Yeah? What's the occasion?"

"It's the day Michael Fountain dies."

"And Miguel Fuentes returns?"

"They'll never let Miguel Fuentes return. They'll kill him."

I pressed the record button. "Who are they?"

Miranda put the tray on the floor and left.

"Maybe you're one of them," Fountain said.

"Maybe I am," I said. "But you'll have to take my word that I'm not."

He smiled under the beard; his teeth were stained with tobacco, and dirt was jammed under the fingernails of his small hands. The hands moved the ice and the glass and the Bacardi bottle in an almost ceremonial way, like a priest preparing for Mass. He lifted an olive and stared at it.

"I don't even know your name," he said.

"Briscoe."

"It doesn't matter, really. I knew you would come here to get me eventually," he said. "And now you've got me."

He popped the olive into his mouth, gnawed at it, moving the pit around in his mouth. When the pit was clean he spat it on the floor.

"I didn't come here to get you," I said. "I want to talk to you about your brother."

"I had two brothers. They're both dead."

"Pepe is alive. I saw him two nights ago."

His eyes darted around. "Pepe is alive? But . . ."

"The plane crash was a fake," I said. "He's alive, probably in Acapulco, and probably about to leave the country."

He sipped the rum, trying to compose himself.

"What do you want to know about him?" he said.

"I want to know about October 1959."

"That."

"Yeah," I said. "Some people have died in the last couple of days. And it goes back to that."

"There isn't much to say," he muttered. "There is little to say, and of course, much to say."

I reached forward with the recorder.

"So talk about it."

He exhaled, and looked at the recorder, and then at me, locking eyes with me. He looked like a man who had been silent for too long.

"Okay," he said.

"As much as you want to say."

"Well, it's not really October you want to hear about," he said. "It really started in August. We were all still together in Havana, but everything was different. One day the *barbudos* came to the factory, told my father he had robbed his last worker, and took over. The foreman was made the head of the factory. For years my father had taken care of him and his family, but on that day he walked over to my father and spat in his face." He shrugged. "I suppose revolutions are like that."

"They usually are," I said. "When they're real revolutions."

"The odd thing was that at first my brother Rafael and I welcomed the revolution. We were for Castro. We thought he was Robin Hood, fighting in the hills. And we knew that Batista was a pig. A torturer. A murderer. At least three of the people I grew up with had been slaughtered by his secret police. So when Fidel won, we had a party. Pepe told us suddenly that he had been working with Fidel all along. He came out that day and waved the flag of Fidel, and soon went off to join the new Air Force."

"What happened in August?"

"I'm getting there," he said. "By August we were poor. My father had nothing. My mother was sick, but the family doctor had already gone to Miami. Rafael was growing more furious by the day, but he didn't know how to do any work. So I supported them all. In New York, when I went to Pratt, I worked after school in an advertising agency and knew how to do paste-ups and mechanicals. So I stopped painting, and did the hack work again, at *Bohemia* magazine. Most of the staff was leaving, and the magazine was soon to die. But I worked there in the final months."

"It was honest work."

"Yes, but it wasn't painting. And I was a painter. Then one night in August, Pepe arrived at the place where we were living. He was in his Air Force uniform. He had a lot of money. He had food. He said we should begin to get ready, because soon we would all be leaving Cuba. He had all the shades down, and the lights low, and later the American came."

"The one with the scar on his cheek?"

"Yes." He seemed surprised. "Yes, that one."

"What was his name?"

"He said his name was Thompson. Like the machine gun, he said, and Pepe laughed. He was about forty, lean, with a sport shirt, hair cut short, always talking with his hand in front of his mouth. He said he got the scar from a machine-gun bullet in Korea, and his manner was . . . seething. He started drinking vodka, straight, and he drank hard. He talked about the need to get rid of Fidel Castro."

"Was he C.I.A.?"

"Pepe never said. I assume he was."

"So . . ."

"So, we had one thing to do before this Thompson would arrange a boat for us to leave."

He sipped the Bacardi, and reached for another ice cube. The cube made a plopping sound. The ice in the bowl was beginning to melt.

"I would have to go to Camaguey," he said. "Pepe was a pilot, operating out of Camaguey. I could go there and wander around painting in the hills, but when I was needed, I would have to act. The family would be taken care of while I was gone. I said I didn't want to be involved in killing anyone. Pepe took me aside and told me that it was too late for that kind of talk. If I did not help, then the family's names would be given to Fidel, and all of us would be put against a wall and shot. All of us."

"You weren't married then?"

"No, but I was in love with someone."

He hesitated, blinked, spat the olive pit hard

across the room. It hit a canvas and dropped to the floor.

"So I agreed. In a way, those weeks were happy, wandering in the hills around the town of Camaguey, doing watercolors and sketches. I felt like an artist again. But then one night Pepe came for me. He gave me a pistol and told me what I must do. In the morning, Fidel would take off on a plane for Havana. Pepe would take off right after him. It was mandatory that the control tower not alert Fidel to the plane that was following. Camaguey is a tiny airport, and there was only one man in the control tower."

"And all you had to do was kill him."

"Yes."

"And you did."

"Yes."

He drained the glass. All the cubes were melted now, and he ran a thick finger through the water.

"Miranda!" he called. There was no answer. "Miranda, *donde està?*" Still no answer. "I guess she went out," he said, shrugging. He leaned all the way back against the wall.

"How did you get away?" I said.

"I walked. The gun had a silencer. I put it under my shirt, and walked out of the tower and into the jungle. I walked for two days until I came to the place where the boat was waiting. Pepe was already gone. He had flown straight to some American Air Force base in Florida. But everyone else was there. They took us out in the darkness and put us on another freighter, bound for Mexico. I didn't even know that it was Camilo Cienfuegos who died until I got to Mexico. Pepe and Thompson were waiting for us in Vera Cruz. They kept saying that they didn't get the top son of a bitch, but they got a big son of a bitch. And I was sick."

He stood up and went over to a mantel and looked at some pictures of all of them in cheap Woolworth frames. Three boys, a mother and father, sitting in the garden of a tropical house. Confirmation.

High school graduation. A gag picture of Miguel, posed at a painter's easel in a beret. I got up and looked at the rest. A Mass card for Rafael, asking God's mercy in Spanish. And a picture of a younger Miguel, thin, beardless, eyes squinting into the harder sun of Mexico, a faint smile, standing with a girl. I didn't know the girl, but I recognized the woman. I had just seen her picture on a phony passport.

"This girl," I said, "this is the girl you loved?"

"Yes. She left Havana before us."

"Her name is Lillian Boney, isn't it? And now she's married to Pepe."

His voice choked, he stepped back, he looked like a man who had just been punched.

"How did . . . "

"I've seen her picture before. She's with Pepe now, in Acapulco, I would imagine. She's going to leave with him."

The recorder clicked, signaling that we had used one side of the cassette. While Miguel stood facing the window, staring moodily into the street, I flipped the cassette over, and turned it on again.

"Why did you break up with her?" I said.

He coughed, cleared his throat, but didn't look me in the eye. "It was because of Pepe. In Mexico, I found it hard to live with what had happened. Pepe didn't care. But I had killed a man. And I knew it was wrong. I knew that killing Fidel would have been wrong too. I was reading everything about Cuba, and every day I learned more about the Batista tyranny. I knew that Fidel was better for Cuba than anything that had gone before, and I said this to Pepe and to my father. They hated me for saying such things, but Pepe was the worst. He said that if I ever talked about any of this outside the family, he would kill me. And he would kill Lillian first. I knew him. I knew he would do it. Soon, I was sick all the time, and not painting, and feeling like killing myself. And so, after the bank was set up, I decided to go away. I took fifty thousand dollars out of the bank, and said

good-bye to Lillian. I tried to explain to her that I
wanted a new life, and that she would be a part of it.
But I would set up that life first, and come for her.
She had to trust me. She had to understand how much
I needed peace, how I had to kill the past. So I became Michael Fountain, the American painter, and
vanished into the Yucatan. I was there a year and a
half. Lillian did not answer my letters. And soon the
isolation was too much for me. I made my way up
here, where there were bookstores and painters and
art supplies. And of course, with so many people
around, I was more isolated than ever."

"And you never saw Lillian again?"

"Yes, I saw her. I was coming back from Yucatan,
with my new beard, and forty pounds heavier, and on
my way to San Miguel, I drove through Mexico City.
Foolish. Like a moth going to the flame. But I wanted
to see her, to tell her that I was alive, that I wanted
her to come with me, to live this life with me. She
wasn't home at her old apartment and I waited in the
car for her. That night, she arrived, walking oddly,
as if she had been drinking, and she was with Pepe.
He was already married to Moya Vargas, the actress.
I hid low in the car, because to be truthful, I feared
him more than I feared anyone else. They went into
the building together. They did not come out."

Now I understood things better. "Is that why
you're telling me all of this?" I said.

"Maybe. Maybe I have a lot of reasons. When I
was still a Catholic, we had what was called a General
Confession. You could make it once a year, or once
every few years, and then you could deal with everything, all the lies and evasions of your life. And it
always made me feel cleaner."

"Do you feel cleaner now?"

"No."

"What would make you feel clean?"

"To kill Pepe. He was the one who ruined my
life."

"Is that why you cried the day you read the story of his death in the *News?*"

He looked at me warily. "You have learned a lot about me, haven't you?"

"Only fragments," I said. "That's the best any reporter can hope to ever find out. Bits. Pieces. And hope that they add up to an approximation of the truth."

He lit a cigar, looking oddly weak and vulnerable, the way his father had looked. And resigned.

"Truth . . ." His voice trailed off.

"You paint well."

"Yes, but what can I do with my work? Suppose I have a show in New York? Suppose it gets a lot of attention, and suppose I become famous? What then? Do they discover that this man was born at age thirty-six in 1964? A man with no youth, no childhood, no adolescence, no family, no parents, no wife or child, not even a fucking dog? Do you see, Briscoe? Do you understand that?"

"And now you want to come out?"

"Now I want the truth. I've grown old running, and I don't care anymore. I don't even want to be famous anymore, or to be respected by critics, or collected by other artists. I just want the boil to break."

He had wandered to the front window, and was staring out into the street. Then his eyes suddenly brightened, and he said, "*Ay dios mio . . .*" And I looked past him. Coming up the street was Miranda. Behind her were two cops, carrying rifles.

22

I switched off the tape recorder, stuffed it into my belt, and followed Miguel across the studio to the back window. He opened the window and looked down two stories.

"Go ahead," he said, "I'll be right behind you."

I dropped to the sandy ground, and looked up. Miguel held a shotgun, which he tossed down to me, and then came out the window legs first, hanging to the ledge with his small soft hands before letting go. When he got up, he was limping.

"Come on," he said. He moved between two houses, skipping and limping, and reached into his belt and took out a .38. Ahead of us was a hill, dotted with boulders and gnarled mountain trees and a steep slope behind it, leading to terraced gardens. I looked behind me and saw one of the cops come out from behind one of the houses, shouting at us, and gesturing with the rifle.

"Follow that road and you'll hit the back of the Art Institute," he said. "Your hotel is straight across the road."

"What about you?"

"My leg is shot. I'll hold them back. I want you to get that tape to someone who can do something about it. If I can stop them, I have a car I can use to get out of here."

He took the shotgun out of my hands, and slipped behind a boulder, as the first rifle shot split the still, late afternoon air.

"Run!" he said.

And run I did, from boulder to boulder, and tree

to tree, while Miguel leaned out from behind his rock,
firing his shotgun and his .38. I turned for one last
look, and saw Miguel lifting a foot into the air, as a
bullet slammed into him. He fell forward onto the
rock, his right hand straight out, firing a final
round.

I dropped into a dry wash and ran, my legs
pumping, my chest aching, a stitch tearing at my side,
holding the tape recorder in my left hand. My eyes
were clogged with dust and then a dog suddenly ap-
peared in front of me, diving at my feet, barking
and biting at my legs. I saw an old man up the slope
to my left, staring impassively, as I yelled and kicked
at the dog. Then ahead, I saw the back of the Art
Institute, and the town spreading away to the right.
I stopped, waited, listened, saw no police cars,
kicked at the dog until he gave up, and hurried into
the back of the Art Institute.

Nobody looked at me as I hurried through, caked
with dust. I guess with the dirt and the anxiety I
looked like just another visiting writer. I stopped at
the front door, looked out at the wide, traffic-clogged
roads, still saw no police cars, and stepped out carefully.

To the left the road rose over a hill, carrying the
heavy trucks to Guanajuato. That was the way I
would go. The other way, up the cobblestoned streets
to the tezontle road that went to Mexico City, was
where the cops would be. I walked casually across the
street, through the gates leading to the hotel, and into
the main building. I smiled at the young girl behind
the desk, told her to get my bill ready for checking
out. Everything in my room was the way I'd left it.
I put the briefcase inside the suitcase, closed it and
carried suitcase and typewriter to the front desk.

Across the street, in front of the Art Institute, was
a police car.

"I'm sorry you could not stay longer," the girl
said brightly.

"So am I," I said.

"We have a big feast here in a few days."

"Maybe I'll come back through."

"It's the Three Kings. It's like your Christmas."

"I wish I could be here for it."

She counted out my change.

"Well," she said, "maybe next year."

The police car was still there. I could not go through the gates without being seen.

"Is there a service road out back?" I asked.

"You mean, behind the hotel?"

"Yes. The view from that side of town is lovely," I said, doing my tourist act. "I'd like to go back there, so I can photograph the hotel and the Art Institute in the same picture."

"Ah, yes. Of course. Well, there *is* a road, around behind the old stable. But it's only dirt, mister."

"If I stayed on that road, where would it come out?"

She chewed on the eraser of a pencil. "Let's see . . . it must come out on the old road. Where do you go from here?"

"To Mexico City."

A cop walked out of the Art Institute, his uniform a daub of baby blue in the dusty road.

"Ah, *bueno*. Well, if you turn right on the old road, you will come to the main road to Mexico. If you go left, it leads to Guanajuato. So don't go left."

"*Muchissimas gracias, señorita.*"

She grinned. "Have a good voyage."

The cop got into the car and drove up the hill behind the endless caravan of trucks. I lifted the bags and went out to the car, and drove around the back to the dirt road. I wondered if any of them knew Miguel—the cops; or Miranda, who had been paid by someone to keep track of his visitors; or any of the young Americans, sitting in the bars, arguing abstractions. His life had changed one morning long ago, and so had a little piece of history, and I had it now on one small cassette. I pulled up on the old road, and headed for Guanajuato.

It was dark when I reached Guanajuato. I checked into the Hotel Florida, and placed a call to Murray at his office in Mexico City. Jaime answered. No, Murray wasn't there. No, he didn't know where Murray was. He must be sick. He hadn't been in all day. I left a number for Murray to call.

I went out, bought a *torta* in an all-night cafe, and washed it down with a cold bottle of Bohemia. Then I found a *farmacia* that was still open and bought two rolls of surgical tape. I went up to the room, took the cassette out of the recorder, wrapped it tightly in paper, taping the ends, and then, watching carefully in the mirror, I taped it to the small of my back. I put a fresh cassette in the recorder. I took the two .45s out of the suitcase and put one under the pillow and the other under the mattress. I went to bed and tossed for a while, examining all the pieces again, and then fell asleep.

Murray called a little before dawn.

"Where the hell's my car?" he said.

"I've got it here. In Guanajuato, Murray. Don't worry about it."

"That's the only thing I ever owned, Briscoe."

"Listen, I need some help," I said, ignoring the car. "Can you do a little reporting?"

"Right now?"

"As soon as you wake up."

"That'll be this afternoon. I'm with Irma."

"Wonderful. I love a good romance."

"What do you want me to do?"

"Find this dame Moya Vargas. She's probably on her way to Acapulco. And she's probably alone."

"I hope so."

"But for Chrissakes, be careful. She's involved in a very heavy deal, which I'll explain to you some other time. And don't worry: I'll get you a good payday."

"I'll see what I can do."

"You know who Moya Vargas is, right, Murray?"

"Hey! I read those clips too, remember? I'd love to boff her."

"No, you wouldn't, Murray."

"I'd like to try anyway."

"I'll call you tonight," I said. "Where you going to be?"

"Try the office. Hey listen . . ."

"Yeah?"

"You didn't kill a chick named Carter, did you?"

"Why do you ask?"

"The cops are looking for a guy who sounds exactly like you. They don't have a name, but they got a description."

"Murray, do I look like the kind of guy who would kill a woman?"

"Yeah."

"Find Moya Vargas, punk. I'll call you tonight."

I hung up and turned on my side and tried to sleep. Nothing happened. They kept moving through my head, like characters from some movie whose reels had been scrambled: Miguel Fuentes, who killed one man and then killed the best part of himself; the girl he once loved, who murdered the memory of Miguel in a compact of betrayal with his brother; the boy, Rafael, shot to pieces in the swamps of the Playa Giron; the mother, dead of a broken heart; the old man, sitting with his cigars and brandy, waiting for death; and Pepe, the bad seed, who had killed more than I would ever know. The family was polluted with death, with the acceptance of it, and the giving. The revolution had arrived in their lives like a brutal summer storm, and they had fallen into a fever whose symptoms were murder and death. None of them would ever recover.

And I knew that they would try to touch me again with their terminal disease. They were out there, the survivors and their agents, and they would keep trying to kill me until they did it right. I just had to get the rest of the story before they got to me. I had to let someone know about all of it. I had to stop Pepe from ever spending that diseased money. And I had to make someone pay. Someone like Moya

Vargas. Someone like Pepe Fuentes. And perhaps
more than all of them, I wanted the American, the
one Miguel called Thompson, the one with the scar
on his cheek, the one who helped to set all these
events in motion. He was somewhere in the world.
In an office in Washington. Or feeding the illusions of
the exiles in Miami. Or off in Greece, listing the vic-
tims for the next round. Or sitting in Chile, sending
notes to the generals. He was somewhere, and I
would make Pepe talk into the tape recorder and tell
about Thompson, and then I would go into a city
room somewhere and write his name on copy paper
with the rest of the story, and wait for the first edition
of that newspaper to come up, and then see whether
they would put him in jail for a long long time. I had
been beaten, shot at, raped and framed. I was goddamned tired of it. And ready to start hurting a lot of
these sons of bitches back.

I got up and brushed my teeth and dressed. I
would sleep in the sun. The plane for Acapulco was at
nine. I could eat somewhere, and then drive out to
the airport and park the car there. I would send the
keys and some money for a plane ticket to Murray
when I was finished.

Driving out to the airport, I felt as alone as I've
ever felt. I was on the run. I would do my best to get
the rest of the story and then try to get out alive.

At the Mexicana counter, I paid cash for a ticket
to Acapulco. The clerk asked for my name and I
told him Faulkner. Guillermo Faulkner. He wrote
it neatly into the name slot on the ticket. I handed
him the suitcase, picked up the typewriter and walked
across the tarmac to the waiting plane.

23

I was in an aisle seat in the first-class cabin and didn't see much of Acapulco as the plane banked for its landing. I glimpsed the famous harbor with its morning beach and its afternoon beach, the dull gleam of the white hotels, the lines sliced in the placid lake of the Pacific by racing boats and water-skiers. The homes of the rich clung precariously to the mountainsides, and I recognized the point of the Quebrada, where the high-divers performed for visiting Americans. One new hotel, built like a giant pyramid, took up most of one of the old beaches. And then the view was gone as the plane dropped behind the mountains to the landing field.

I rode into town with the cab windows open. It was hot. Sticky, silent, oppressive, hot. The palm trees drooped. The foliage seemed to be waiting for something to happen. And I remembered the town when I was young, when there were still great open stretches of beach and you could rent a hammock for a peso a night and in the mornings we would watch the fishermen gutting sharks. Now it was all Pizza Hut, Frankie's Tastee Freeze, Denny's, Kelly's Hamburgers, Sam's Roast Beef Sandwich and all the other plastic monsters that had come vomiting out of the throat of Southern California, like some final humiliating act in the Mexican War. We drove along the Paseo Aleman, and I looked past a hundred thousand stenographers, teachers and airline stewardesses at the still-lovely bay. Away off, clouds were gathering darkly, and there was no wind.

The room at the Hotel Caleta was damp, and

the bed smelled stale. I over-tipped the boy and
opened the blinds, and flicked a switch that started
the ceiling fan. We were on the Mexican side of the
resort town. The fan whined, beating at the stale air.
Sweat began to trickle down my back and chest. I
locked the door, and ripped the cassette off my back,
the adhesive tape tearing out the small hairs. I stood
shirtless under the hot breath of the fan, trying to get
dry, but nothing happened. I wished I were back in
New York, with the snow piling on the skylight and
Red Emma waiting for spring.

I put the two .45s on the bed, covered them with
my jacket and went back to the window. The air
smelled of things frying. The clouds on the horizon
were trying to form thunderheads. Away off, a speed-
boat cut through the sea, riding the long slow hills,
heading for shore. I turned away, sat on the bed and
picked up the phone.

I asked the operator to get me Murray at his office
in Mexico City.

He wasn't there.

Murray, Jaime told me, was in Acapulco. Where
in Acapulco? Las Brisas. Thanks, Jaime. I called the
Las Brisas Hotel, one of the fanciest joints in the
city. I had read about it in travel magazines for years.
When I was a kid in Mexico, the Las Brisas Hotel
had not yet been built.

Yes, a cool unaccented voice said, Murray had
checked in that morning, but no, he wasn't in his
room. I left word for him to call Mr. Faulkner at the
Hotel Caleta, and she said she would give him the
message.

Then I lay down in the slippery heat thinking
that when it got dark I would go around to the Casa
Azul, in the point beyond the Caleta. The place where
Pepe lived. The place where all of them must be, now
that all was finished in Mexico City. If they still had
that $200,000,000 they might have it in the Casa Azul.
Murder was. A lot of murder. I fell asleep.

The phone rang at a little after four.

"*Mis*ter Faulkner."

"Hi, Murray."

"God, I loved *Intruder in the Dust*. One of your best. Almost as good as *Tender Is the Night,* that book you wrote after *A Farewell to Arms*."

"Where are you, Murray?"

"In a town called Ixtapoc." He spelled it for me. "It's up the coast about twelve, thirteen miles. Moya Vargas is here, in a house out on the edge of town. Nice little house, painted white and trimmed in red. There's a little dock at the bottom of a cliff. And some guys hanging around with guns. They keep looking out to sea, like waiting for a boat or something."

"Beautiful."

"I got her Mexico City address from a friend of Irma's," he said, sounding pleased. "You know, hookers know everything. I figured I'd take a look, just in case she didn't leave yet for the Big A. I rented a car from Avis and went to her house, out in San Angel, an expensive-looking joint. She and two guys were just coming out, and they were carrying a ton of luggage, including a big silver trunk, so I figure right away they are going someplace. They are. Or at least she is. Right to the fucking airport. So I ditch the car at the Avis fast-check-in counter, and walk over and see where she's going. Acapulco. Beautiful. I get a ticket too, and reserve another car in Acapulco. The two *mozos* bow and leave, and me and Moya get on the plane, sixty-three passengers apart. We get here forty-five minutes later, and while she waits for this shitload of luggage, I get another car. And I wait."

"Pretty good, Murray."

"Well, the porters load the trunk and the other shit in the car, and she heads right for Las Brisas. In a limo with Mexican plates. I got the number written down. But they don't unload the limo at Las Brisas. She is not staying there. Instead, this Vargas broad goes into the bar. When she does that I check in. They give me a beef because I don't have luggage, and I don't have a reservation, but I call for the public relations guy and show him my press card and give him the I'm-from-a-wire-service-and-we-have-1,500-newspapers act, and he finds me a room. I get the key and go out to the lobby and after a while, the Vargas dame comes out of the bar with an American. And I follow them out here."

"Did he have a scar on his cheek? The American?"

"As a matter of fact, yeah."

"Touchdown," I said.

"What the hell is this about?" Murray said.

"I'll tell you when I see you. And hey, listen, where are you anyway? . . ."

"I'm in a Pemex station, across the road from the joint where Vargas went with the big silver trunk . . ."

"I'll catch up to you later."

"Hey, just a second!"

"What is it, Murray?"

"Where's my fuckin' car?"

"I ate it, Murray," I said, and hung up, thinking, kid, you are a hell of a reporter.

The manager of the Hornos boat dock made me show my passport and tourist card when I rented the fishing boat, but I didn't care any more about hiding my name or leaving a trail. I was going somewhere that the cops couldn't go for a while. The boat was called the *Esmeralda*, twenty-one feet long with twin Mercs and extra gas tanks, fully equipped with poles and gear. The sad-eyed middle-aged manager looked out at the darkness on the horizon, and murmured that it didn't look good for fishing, but I told him the weather report said the storm was heading north, and I just wanted to take it out today, get the feel of it, then lash it up for the night and start fishing early in the morning. His face remained dubious, but he took my money, and gassed the boat while I loaded my suitcase and typewriter aboard. I was wearing white trousers, sneakers, and a blue knit crew shirt, so I must have looked sufficiently sporty, or sufficiently prosperous, to be a good bet.

The manager shouted orders to two dock boys and they untied the lines and shoved me off and I waved to them from the foam rubber seat and was off. There was a heavy chop. Sea birds chattered their warnings. The sky grew darker. I moved out into the harbor and pushed the burbling engines. They would do forty knots if they had to, but I kept the speed down to twenty-five, angling over to starboard, heading out past the point. I could see a blue house perched on the point. The Casa Azul. There was a launch tied to a dock at the bottom of the cliff, and a cluster of fishing boats resting like white birds on the sea, and all the while these   ng blue rollers kept coming in faster from out there in the Pacific, rolling from Hawaii, rolling from the Philippines, full of warning and wet menace, telling of the storm.

I went out behind the cluster of fishing boats and cut the engines and drifted for a while. There were glasses in the utility compartment and I trained them on the point. I could see three men lounging on the dock beside the launch, and not much going on, except that other men were coming down a stone pathway from the cliff above, carrying packages. They were clearing out, and they were taking everything they could carry.

They loaded the launch and then someone took it out to a yacht that lay at anchor far beyond the fishing boats. A white cruiser deep in the rolling sea. I put the glasses on it. The yacht was very big. Big enough to go a long way away. The ladder was on the other side and I couldn't see them unloading. Then the launch returned empty to the dock and filled up again and went back to the cruiser. There were two more trips and then they were finished.

On the last trip back, the launch was lashed to the
dock and three of the men stayed there. Then the
cruiser lifted anchor and began to move. Heading
south. I waited a long time before starting after it.
There was no hurry. A cruiser that large would not be
easy to hide.

They went south to another rocky point, jutting
out from the land, anchored and waited for a launch.
I went past them, more than half a mile away, keeping low, trying not to attract attention, just putt-putt-
ing along. The launch pulled up and some figures
went down a ladder from the yacht and boarded the
launch. I cut the engines and pretended to fish. With
my hands out of view, I taped the cassette to the inside of a life belt, addressed it to Harvey Matofsky
at the *Post* in New York, and then pulled on the life
belt and laced it up. Lightning scribbled across the
distant sky. Lying low, letting the fishing pole bob
in its clamps, I put glasses on the mainland.

Several *pistoleros* lounged on the dock and there
were steps leading up to a tree-protected house built
on the shoulder of a mountain that fell away to the
sea. Over to the right, a fishing village lay huddled
at the junction of two mountains. Behind the village,
about two miles, and standing like a giant wall sealing
off the interior, was a dam.

I turned back to the dock just as the *pistoleros*
turned suddenly and looked up, as if they had heard
something. Out on the ocean, I heard nothing. They
looked up the path, and then turned to talk to each
other again. One of them lit a cigarette. I could see
the palms on the cliff begin to sway from the rising
breeze. There were more whitecaps on the sea.

Then two *pistoleros* came down the stone steps
carrying a body to the dock. The others helped tie
something to the body. They dumped it heavily into
the launch, and two of them climbed in. They started
out through the chop, cleaving a trail of foam through
the darkening water. They went out past the yacht,

heading for deep water. Then they slowed, as if the engine were idling. The two men lifted the body. I could see more clearly now, as they heaved and swung and dropped the weighted body into the water.

It was Murray.

24

I moved the boat around to the right, just south of the fishing village, and waited for night. The people on the yacht were waiting too. The lights went on, and from the distance I could see a phosphorescent trail as the launch moved back and forth from the dock. The weather was changing and my boat began to rise and fall. There was more lightning now, and the shapes of the mountains looked huge in the darkness, and then the wind started blowing harder, and suddenly all the lights went out in the fishing village. Just like that. As if the village had been snuffed out of existence. I had the .45s wrapped in oilcloth under one side of the life jacket and the tape recorder under the other. Everything was darkness now, with the moon gone behind clouds and the village dark and the stars vanished. All dark, except for the yacht and the dull distant glow of Acapulco to the north.

It was time to move.

I took the *Esmeralda* through the heavy chop, the running lights out, the engines barely moving. Waves lifted me and dropped me, and my teeth banged against each other, and something rattled loosely in the engine, but the yacht kept getting bigger.

And then suddenly everything grew calm.

The wind stopped.

The sea grew sullen and smooth.

Even the lightning ceased in the distance.

The yacht was fifty yards away, high and white and powerful, like a building floating in the sea. I left my boat moving, heading away from the yacht, then

slipped over the side and began to swim. I stayed
underwater until my lungs ached, came up for air and
location, and went under again. The last time I came
up, I was certain they would see me. The boat was
lit up like a Christmas tree. At the stern, tied with a
rope, was a dinghy. Now they could not see me from
the yacht.

I heard someone above me shouting orders in
Spanish, and the cranking of the anchor chain, the
anchor rising out of the water with a whooshing
sound, and when I looked up the lights on deck were
out. They were about to cast off.

"Captain, captain, what about the dinghy, sir?"
someone shouted.

"Cut it loose."

I went under again, felt the taut dinghy line go
loose, and dove for the hull. The yacht was being
turned around, and the water swirled around me, and
I thought I would never come up, and then came up,
bumping along the hull, and found myself a few
feet from the ladder. I reached for it and was
bumped again, as the yacht continued its turn, and
then put my feet against the side and pushed out
against the turn, reaching through the darkness of the
water, and grabbed the bottom rung. I held on, under
the water line, while the yacht continued the turn,
and then felt the huge boat start moving forward. I
pulled myself out of the water, patted myself, felt
the guns and the recorder, and then started up the
ladder.

I came out on an empty teak deck, cabins to the
left, a rail to the right. The curtains were drawn on
all the cabin portholes, but were not perfectly aligned.
I eased up to the stern porthole and peeked in. Don
Luis was alone, dozing in a large chair, an open book
in his hand.

The second cabin was larger inside, clearly a cabin
built for people who own things. My view was
blocked by the back of Pepe's head. I was so close
that I could count the hairs. Pepe's neck and shoulders

were bare, but I couldn't tell whether the rest of him was naked too. It didn't much matter. Pepe was staring at the large double-sized bunk against the far wall. So was I. On the bed were his first and second wives. Moya Vargas and Lillian Boney. They were naked. A taut tan body and a looser blonder body. They were entwined and moving and doing things to each other. There were a lot of bottles on a table, as if they had all been on board for a long time now. Against the bulkhead beside the door was a silver trunk. And Pepe did not move.

Two men sat at a table in the third cabin. One of them was young, his hair neatly combed, dressed in a business suit. He looked like the kind of young man who worked as a driver for politicians during political campaigns: blank, and willing, and ambitious, and probably fanatic. The other was older, with hair the color of ashes, a web of wrinkles on his tanned, bony face, and a scar across his cheekbone. This was Thompson. She must have cut him into the big jackpot, now that Lloyd was gone. He was wearing a dark blue shirt, suspenders, a bow tie, and a .45 in a shoulder holster. The two of them were drinking whiskey and talking.

I stepped away from the porthole, and bumped into a young Mexican in a sailor suit. He started to say something. I put the .45 to his chest.

"Can you swim?" I said in Spanish.

He shook his head yes.

I pointed to the sea. "Then swim."

He looked at the still water, and the town passing on the left. It was about a 500-yard swim.

"Go."

He slipped over the side.

I moved to the bridge. An older Mexican in a mate's uniform saw me coming in. He opened his mouth to protest and I knocked him down with the butt of the .45. The captain, a small uniformed version of Gilbert Roland, all braid and moustached charm, looked scared.

"What do you want?" he said, in a heavy accent.

"I want you to move this boat in a circle," I said. "A long slow circle. Nice and easy, so nobody will notice."

"I have orders to go south."

"There is a storm coming. Very soon."

"I know."

"I don't want you to sail this boat into that storm. I want these people alive."

"Are you the police?"

"I have a gun. And I'm prepared to kill you. That's all you have to know about me."

He must have believed me. He slowed the yacht gradually, and started a turn.

I went to the third cabin first to deal with Thompson. I took out the second .45. It might have looked dumb but there were, after all, two of them. I yanked the door and stepped in.

"What the hell . . ."

"Don't make a move, Thompson, or I'll blow your fuckin' face off."

He stood very still. The younger one looked pale and sick.

"You," I said to the younger one. "Stand up." He stood up. "Lift your jacket." He did. No gun. "Lift your trouser bottoms." No gun there either. "Now take the gun off Scarface here. Very easy." He did. The door was open, with the deck and the sea beyond. "Now throw it out there." He threw the gun through the open door into the sea.

"You're a bright boy," I said. The young man looked scared, but not very bright. "Now close the door."

"You must be Briscoe," Thompson said.

"Nah, I'm Richard Harding Davis—you know, the retired literary agent."

I closed the door. "You're playing around with the wrong people, Briscoe," Thompson said. "And for the wrong reasons."

"I'm sure I am," I said. I slipped one of the .45s

back into my belt. Then I took out the tape recorder, unwrapped it, and put it on a table. "I want you to talk to me in a minute," I said. "So keep your pipes oiled."

Without another word, I slammed the young one in the head with the gun and knocked him down. He fell hard.

"You come with me," I said to Thompson. He stood very still.

"You're crazy," he said. "You don't know what you're getting into, boy."

"I know exactly what I'm into, Thompson. I have poor Miguel Fuentes on tape, telling what happened that day you knocked off Camilo Cienfuegos. It should make interesting listening in the White House, pal. And now I've got you here on a boat full of thieves and killers. Cutting yourself into the jackpot. Perfect for an employee of the United States government. Why don't you tell me about it, pal? Why don't you make a speech explaining how you're doing all this for your country?"

"I'll never tell you anything, Briscoe."

I heard a long low rumble a ways off.

"Maybe it doesn't matter. Killing never meant anything to you people, so why should thievery? They let you walk around the world with guns so long you don't even remember all of it. But I think you better tell me what you do remember."

"I won't tell you a thing."

"Good. That means I'll have to kill you. I have five or six good reasons now."

He smirked, the way all those people smirk when they talk to someone whose politics are not theirs. We were soft and naive, and they were hard and clear-eyed. We were to be smirked at.

"Then shoot," he said.

And I did.

Right in the kneecap, the sound of the .45 gigantic in the metal-walled room, and he fell, his eyes wide with surprise and shock and pain. I walked over, stood over him, and shot his other kneecap off. Then I opened the door, grabbed the recorder, and hurried to the next cabin. The door was locked. I shot the lock off and kicked it in.

Pepe was pulling on his trousers when I burst in, and his eyes were large and startled.

Lillian put her hands on her breasts and flattened herself against the wall.

Moya did not move. She lay on her back and stared at me. A faint damp odor came off her, as familiar as morning, and the long dark hard body was gleaming with sweat.

"Hello, Briscoe, come and join the party."

"Shut up," I said.

Pepe zippered his fly. His mouth was working, and his eyes went to the silver trunk against the wall beside the door.

"You're crazy," he said. "You'll never get off this boat alive."

"Maybe not," I said. I pressed the record button on the tape recorder. "But before I go out, I want you to do a little talking, Pepe."

"Stop acting like a boy, Briscoe," Moya said.

"Shut up, Moya," I said. Lillian moved slightly, trying to get farther away from Moya. Her liquid eyes were searching for an attitude, but just looked empty and guilty.

"What do you want to talk about?" Pepe said.

"Let's start with October 1959," I said. The wind was rising now. I could feel the sea slapping against the hull of the yacht as the captain completed his turn. The town was to our right now, out there in the darkness. Pepe's face was the color of oatmeal.

"I don't know what you mean," he said.

"I mean what happened in Camaguey that morning, Pepe. I mean what happened to Camilo Cienfuegos, who died because you thought he was Fidel. I want to know about that, Pepe. I want to know about Anne Fletcher, too. The way you played with her, and romanced her, and then killed her. I want to know about the looting of the New York Bank and Trust, and your political friends in New York, and the way you got the bank in Mexico, and who you did business with there, and how you looted that one too. Tell me how you betrayed your brother Miguel. And tell me what you just did to Murray Peters, a hell of a nice kid, and a goddamned good reporter. He's the kid you killed and dropped in the bay an hour ago, boy. I want to know about all the *dead people*, Pepe."

Lillian screamed, and started out of the bed.

"It wasn't him," she sobbed. "It wasn't Pepe! Or Miguel!" She turned to Moya, who was getting dressed. "It was her! With her big movie-star dreams! *She* made him do it! She divorced him because he wouldn't give her what she wanted. But she never got out of his life, or *mine!* Pepe didn't kill the girl in New York! *She* did! She encouraged that girl to collect all those papers, to bring pressure on Pepe, to talk about going to the press. She didn't think the girl would do anything, and then, after Pepe acted first, after Pepe faked his own death and left, the girl decided to act anyway. And so Moya killed her. She did it. She made us do what *she* wanted. She made me do . . ."

The woman shuddered and stood there unsteadily, her body sagging; you could see what she would be in old age, thick and broken. I turned to Moya. She was smiling thinly. "Calm yourself, Lillian," she said.

The boat rose and fell more sharply now, and the slapping of the sea had become a thumping. Moya was dressed now. She took a cigarette from a pack lying on the table beside the bunk and lit it for herself with a gold lighter.

"But it's true!" Lillian said, almost pleading with me to believe her. She was trying to cover her nakedness now, reaching for sheets and pillows. "Miguel told me the whole story when he left me. I loved him. But he left, he went away, he disappeared."

"What did you marry this bum for anyway?" I said, gesturing at Pepe with the .45.

Moya stepped between me and Lillian, and took a drag on the cigarette.

"Because that was the only way for Pepe to keep her quiet," she said coolly. "It's as simple as that. Pepe knew that if he had Lillian killed Miguel would come for him. Perhaps that was the real tragedy. They were the actors, not me."

She smiled ironically and took a drag on the cigarette. Pepe glanced at me, at her, at the silver trunk. Moya angled around and sat on the trunk.

"Pepe is a weak fool," she said. "He would follow anything with a cunt. Or almost anything. And he had been after Lillian from the day Miguel first brought her around. The first night they met, he made a pass at her, right, Pepe?" Pepe didn't respond. "And Miguel didn't even suspect. Poor innocent, dumb Miguel."

Lillian looked shocked. "You knew that?"

"Pepe always told me everything. We were partners after we stopped being lovers. He even told me when it was time for us to get divorced, so he could marry you."

Lillian started to cry. She buried her head in a pillow, her pink naked body heaving with sobs. I picked a blanket off the floor and tossed it to her.

Moya looked at me steadily. She tamped the cigarette out on the floor. Then:

"Now, let's get down to *business*, Briscoe. We have almost two hundred million dollars on this yacht, and we have to get it out of this country. After the holiday is finished, the police will discover there is no longer a Banco de Maya. You are a two-bit over-the-hill reporter. So we should speak of practical matters. Nothing more." She smiled and said: "How would you like ten million dollars?"

"How would you like to lose your teeth?"

We never finished the chat. Suddenly the yacht lifted, seemed to be suspended in air, and then fell hard, tipping us all against the bulkhead. Lillian was rolling on the floor, her soft body thumping around. Another wave hit and the yacht tipped the other

way. Pepe rushed me, grabbing for the gun. I brought
my knee up hard to his groin and ripped at him with
the gun, and he groaned and then I spun away again,
against the bed, the life jacket cushioning me from
sharp edges, and when I righted myself my gun was
gone.

It was on the floor sliding away from me.

Moya leaped for it.

I leaped for her.

And then the ship was smashed and water
poured through all the sprung portholes and the lights
went out and we were all scrambling in the water near
the door. The gun fired. BLAM. And again. BLAM.
And then we were hit once more and there was no
more shooting and I was lifted and bounced off the
ceiling, and fell again, and was under water, choking.
I came up and the sky split open as lightning lit up
the world, and I saw Lillian lying face down, with a
hole in her back. Pepe and Moya were gone. So was
the silver trunk.

I took the other .45 out of my belt, and stepped
outside, the yacht pitching and tossing. The wind
was rising, pushing the sea before it. I couldn't see the
town.

I heard a shot. Then another shot.

The boat strained over on its side, and I held to
the railing, and then I heard the wind: a long low
ferocious howl, blowing flat across the sea, driving everything before it. The force was elemental, furious,
brutal, as wild and hard as evil. I thought the boat
would go over. But something held it up, something
turned it, something aimed it at the shore. I moved
past Thompson's cabin. The door was open and banging hard. The room was empty. Then I remembered
Don Luis. I jammed the gun back inside the jacket
and moved to his room, pulling myself hand over hand
along the railings. One section of railing came off in
my hand, and I twisted, lurched and started into the
sea, grabbed for a strut, a brace, some piece of old
teak, found it, held on, and saved myself. I swung

around against the bulkhead and found the railing
again. The door to Don Luis' cabin was shut. I jerked
at it, banged on it, but could not get it open. I looked
in through the porthole.

Don Luis was sitting on the floor, a small frail
man, in water up to his waist. Water was coming in
through the far porthole, but he just sat there. I hit
the porthole glass with the handle of the .45, and he
looked up. I waved at him, pointing at the locked
door. He stared at me. I banged again, and signaled
for him to leave.

He smiled.

He shook his head.

And he sat there. He looked unbelievably, beauti-
fully, blissfully happy.

I turned and looked down the deck, as the wind
howled, and saw Thompson's young friend step out of
the captain's bridge, looking panicky and confused.
He saw me. He reached inside his jacket for a gun,
lost his balance, and fell into the gray roaring sea.
The wind was screaming now. I saw a skiff go by,
tumbling hard, end over end, like a child's toy.

When I looked up, the village had grown larger.
There was another lightning flash, and I saw cars up
on end, rooftops lifting, a boy tossed by the pulveriz-
ing wind. The sea was rising and falling in great gray
hills now, the yacht was riding them, out of control,
tossed and grabbed and pulled, and the wind was
screaming, as if its throat were full of all the dead of
all the oceans, full of all those who had chased trea-
sures and the sun and great white whales. The yacht
was almost certain to run aground, to be crushed
against the sea wall, to pile into the dense tangle of
smaller boats. I was almost certain I would die.

But I had to finish this. If Moya Vargas was on
this yacht, I had to find her. I had to find Pepe. I had
to find Thompson. I wanted them alive.

I started again for the bridge.

Pepe was at the wheel, twirling it frantically, trying to steer a course away from the sea wall onto the

beach, and when I stepped into view I saw the other two. Thompson was lashed to a stationary chair, a rifle in his hands, his ruined legs flapping in their stained trousers. His face was drained and dim. Moya had one arm hooked into the back of Pepe's belt. She had a .38 in her free hand.

"You lousy bastard!" she shouted at me. "You ruined it for us! You screwed it all up!" She tried to get the gun around. She was too slow. I got out of the way, as Thompson fired the rifle at me, splintering part of the door frame. I slipped on the tossing deck. Another round. Then another. The frame splintering. I held to a stanchion.

"Too bad, Briscoe!" Thompson shouted. "You're gonna die, we're all gonna die! There's no one left, Briscoe, you dumb son of a bitch!"

"Shut up, shut up!" Pepe yelled.

I leaned around for a peek, staying very low, and Thompson fired again, too high, and I reached in and fired at him.

And then there was a long scraping ripping sound, and we were being torn open by something under us, and I rolled and dove. The wind laughed, roared, screamed.

And then I was in the silence of the sea.

25

I came up on the littered beach on the far side of
the tiny harbor. Palm trees were flattened out. Fishing
shacks were piled like driftwood against the up-
rooted tree line. I rolled, staying low, and the waves
kept pounding in, driving me forward, then sucking
me back to the sea. Each time I drove my arms
deeper into the sand, to wait out the undertow. The
second .45 was gone. I reached around and felt my
back. Under the life vest the cassette was still there.

I rolled until I hit the tree line, and then, free
of the salty teeth of the sea, I looked back. The yacht
was broken, impaled on a reef to the left of the harbor. The sea had leaped the wall and was pouring
into the town. I stepped on something. A chicken,
denuded of all its feathers. I moved toward the town,
and saw two giant toppled trees, one pushed through
the roof of a house, the other crushing a milk truck.
A railroad car lay on its side beside the blasted station. I saw dead cats, dogs, and children broken by
the twisting, grinding force of the wind.

I came around one gutted house and looked into
the main street of the town. A giant Pepsi-Cola sign
had fallen through the roof of the post office. Cars
were on their backs like wounded turtles, and a shrimp
boat lay on its side in front of a bakery. There were
no lights and the streets were covered with a glassy
wind-driven sheen. I looked up and saw the giant form
of the dam, two miles away.

Then a block further, I saw Pepe and Moya. He
was bare chested. She had on dungarees and a man's
shirt. They were on either side of the silver trunk,
moving slowly with its great weight, heading for a

huge flatbed truck. I felt naked without the gun. An awning tore off the front of a butcher shop and went banging up the street, and Moya turned into the howling wind and saw me. They looked like lovers caught in the act of eloping.

She said something, and Pepe turned. And they put the trunk down in the middle of the street, and he took a step forward, and raised his arm straight out and fired. I saw the muzzle flash, but heard nothing in the wind. I fell to the side into the doorway of a stone building. I jiggled the tin-covered door. Another shot rang out, chipping away a hunk of stone, and the door gave in, and I was in a room, filled with Mexican women and small crying children. The wind howled behind me, and I could not get the door closed, and then I was going out the back door, slamming it behind me, and saw a hole blown through the boards of the door. Pepe was in there now.

I stopped running.

And waited.

I looked up into the hills and saw the steeple of a church jiggle, totter and then break away, shaved off cleanly by the razor of the wind, its bells tolling forlornly as it blew into the jungle.

Pepe came through the door.

I leaped on him, grabbing for the gun, jamming my thumb between the two large knuckles of the gun hand, feeling him toss, snarl, growl, no words spoken, just animal anger and desperation, as he clutched at my throat with the fingers of his free hand, scratching, clawing at me, trying to bite me, but not able to get a grip. Until his hand opened. And the gun fell. And I spun him, and threw a right hand into his groin, and then a hook deep into the soft belly, and came up with a right hand to the chin, bouncing his head off the wall of the building, then bending, snapping my head up hard to his chin, and dropping one final hook on him before he fell wheezing to the rain-soaked ground.

I grabbed the gun and went quickly along behind

the buildings, circling around to the main street, looking for Moya.

The silver trunk lay in the middle of the rainlashed street.

Moya was nowhere in sight.

"Moya!" I called. "Come out, Moya!"

The wind howled. And I was afraid. Somewhere out at sea was the wave. It came with every hurricane. It could be twenty-five feet high. Higher. And if it came, and drove hard enough through this village and up that narrow valley and hit that dam, all of it would come down.

"Moya," I shouted at the wind. "It's over! You can't go anywhere now! Moya!"

I looked up to the right and thought I saw a flash of light, from somewhere behind the village. Perhaps it's the soldiers, I thought. Coming to evacuate the town. Or the police. No. It would not be the police. The soldiers.

"Briscoe!"

She was coming out of a doorway across the street. She had a little girl in front of her, as a shield, and she was holding a .38 to the little girl's head.

"You're going to help me," she said. "You're going to put that trunk in that truck for me, Briscoe. You are going to put it in that truck now. Or I'll kill this girl."

Her eyes were wild, her hair plastered flat against the oval skull, her clothes glued to the lean body. The little girl was wearing a red dress, and looked terrified.

"I can't do that, Moya," I said. "It'll be easier if you just come with me to the police."

"You only have a few seconds, Briscoe."

She never even asked about Pepe. A woman came out of a doorway and started to plead and scream for her little daughter's life. I tried to figure the chances of hitting Moya with a shot before she killed the girl. They didn't exist.

I put Pepe's gun in my belt.

"No," she shouted. "On the ground."

I took it out and dropped it on the ground. I went over to the trunk and slowly began dragging it to the truck. As long as I was doing this, I would be alive. When I had finished she would kill me. Or she would certainly try. It was as simple as that. But none of this concerned that little girl. There were too many dead already. I didn't want to add still another to the dismal list. I kept my back to the truck so I could watch her, and as I dragged the trunk, she moved, maintaining about fifteen feet between us. The little girl had black obsidian Indian eyes and she didn't understand anything at all. Then the child's mother screamed and pointed at the line of buildings to my left.

Staggering and hurt, his face bloody and pulpy from the beating, battered by the wind, came Pepe.

"Stay back!" Moya shouted at him.

But he kept coming.

Right at me.

"Get back, Pepe! I . . ."

She took the gun away from the girl's head for a moment and the girl bolted, and she turned to aim at the girl, and Pepe was still coming, and she looked at me, and started to aim at me, and then, roaring into the village came a Jeep. It was coming very fast. She saw who was driving it, and she fired. Blam. And—blam! Three shots. And the windshield splintered and the Jeep kept coming, and she fired again. And here it came, and she started to fire again and it ran right into her. Tossing her high in the air. Breaking her.

Miguel got out of the car. His shirt was open and his chest was bandaged. He looked over at his brother and at me and at Moya's broken body.

And he reached into the Jeep.

Away off, a long loud roar started in the throat of the sea.

He took out a rifle.

And I could see a mountain moving in from the sea. Away off. As wide as the world.

He aimed the rifle at Pepe. I started to run over.

"Miguel, don't kill him. Keep him alive."

"No. I traveled two days coming here. Knew they'd end here. Knew it would end here. Knew they'd all come here. Somewhere around here. Told me at the Casa Azul. Told me up there at Moya's house on the point. Lillian was with him, right? Right. Well, now I'm gonna kill him."

"Don't."

"Sorry. Should've done this a long time ago."

Pepe stood in the street, swaying and hurt. Miguel lifted the rifle, ready to execute his brother. I batted the rifle away. The shot went careening down the street.

And then we all turned to look at the sea.

At the wall coming in at us.

Black and dark.

Forty feet high. Fifty. Carrying all before it. Immense. It was the sea. It fell on us.

26

They found me naked on the slope of a hill, high above the valley. A light rain fell steadily. One of the soldiers was very young, and the older man told him to go to the trucks and get a blanket, and a stretcher too, if I needed it. The sun was shining. I told him I did not need a stretcher and then I tried to get up and fell back and he said I would need a stretcher and I said yes, you are right.

More soldiers came, their boots thick with mud, and they wrapped me in a blanket and put me on a truck. I looked down in the direction of the sea. There was a jagged hole where the dam had been. And a great clean bald valley had been carved out of the place where the old valley had been. It was as if the skin of the earth had been ripped away and replaced with something new and primitive and untouched by men. The town was gone. The yacht was gone. The trunk with all that money was gone. Pepe was gone. Moya was gone. Don Luis was gone. Thompson was gone. Miguel was gone. The little girl in the red dress was gone. My clothes were gone. And the cassette was gone.

"You are North American?" a sergeant said.

"Yes," I said. "I was fishing when the storm hit."

"You are lucky."

"Yes."

"They are evacuating the Americans from Acapulco," he said.

"I have no papers. As you can see."

He smiled. "I can see. It does not matter. In such an emergency, such things are of no importance."

"Was Acapulco badly hurt?"

"No. The storm just missed. The worst part hit here. Three hundred people are missing. The dam broke, you see. In Acapulco, they are calling it a miracle."

"It is a miracle. For Acapulco."

"What happened to you?" he said.

"There is no point in telling. Nobody would believe it."

"How are you called?"

"Ishmael," I said, laughing. "Call me Ishmael."

He helped lift me into the army truck. There were a lot of people lying in the back. Children. Old men. Fishermen. As the truck climbed up the ridge to the road, I looked out at the still glass lake of the Pacific. Some of what had happened came to me, some of the past few days, some of what I now knew had happened to a lot of people, years ago, when I was young. I pushed all of those things out of my head. I stared at the gray sky and dozed, hurting when the truck hit a bump.

As we reached the crest and pulled onto the main road, the sky shifted, and the sun broke it open, throwing its rays on the wounded earth. I turned away, aching and hurt, longing for the snows of New York.